Praise for
SUSAN SHREVE'S
Blister

★ "With a tightly woven plot, entirely convincing characters and flashes of humor from the determined 10-year-old narrator, Shreve again proves herself an inspired and inspiring storyteller."
—*Publishers Weekly,* starred review

■ "This perceptively written novel with memorable characters (Blister's grandmother is an original) gets right to the bone."
—*Booklist,* boxed review

"Spunky and resolute, Blister is a character many readers will understand intimately."
—*Kirkus Reviews*

"This is a nuanced and effective examination of a girl who finds both the extent and the limits of her strength."
—*Bulletin of the Center for Children's Books*

"Fans of 'resilience' literature be warned: There's nothing sweet or sentimental about this tart young heroine's story."
— *Washington Post*

"Anyone who has ever done the wrong thing for the right reasons will appreciate [Blister's] wry humor and real life idiosyncrasies. An enormously appealing, marvelously crafted story."
—*Book Sense 76*

Λ *Publishers Weekly* Best Children's Book of 2001

A Children's *Book Sense 76* Selection

An ALA Notable Book

Other Signature Titles

*Jonah the Whale and How He
Became Incredibly Famous*
Susan Shreve

Ghost Cats
Susan Shreve

Bad Girls
Cynthia Voigt

Bat 6
Virginia Euwer Wolff

P.S. Longer Letter Later
Ann M. Martin and Paula Danziger

The Music of Dolphins
Karen Hesse

Out of the Dust
Karen Hesse

BLISTER

SCHOLASTIC SIGNATURE
AN IMPRINT OF SCHOLASTIC INC.

New York Toronto London Auckland Sydney
Mexico City New Delhi Hong Kong Buenos Aires

BLISTER

trouble

Susan Shreve

To Lily and Rebecca Salky
-S.S.

ISBN 0-439-19314-1

12 11 10 9   4 5 6 7/0

Printed in the U.S.A.   40

First Scholastic paperback printing, September 2002

Original hardcover edition designed by Elizabeth B. Parisi, published by Arthur A. Levine Books, an imprint of Scholastic Press, September 2001

CHAPTER ONE

The morning the Reeds' baby died was June 5: a day shimmering with light, the smell of lilacs hanging sweetly in the willow tree behind the house where Alyssa was hiding. From the tree, Alyssa could see the house where she lived, a yellow clapboard house with dark-green shutters, purple clematis climbing the front to the second-story window.

No one even knew or seemed to care that she was missing. Not her father, Jack

Reed, who had arrived full of bad temper from the hospital in his old truck. Nor Daisy G., Alyssa's grandmother — the dance champion of New Haven, Connecticut, in the "Seventy and Over" category — who was waiting for Alyssa's father on the front porch with a cup of coffee. She put her arm around his shoulder and they walked into the house, where the telephone was ringing.

Alyssa had watched her parents leave for the hospital in the middle of the night — leaning out the window of her bedroom as they got into the truck. Her mother, a belly huge with the new baby, was illuminated by the moon, bathed in silver light so her hair glittered and she seemed to float. That was the last Alyssa saw of her — an angel climbing into a pickup truck.

The next morning her father called from the hospital.

"Give me Daisy G.," he'd said, when Alyssa answered the phone.

They knew the baby was a girl. Already she had been given a name — Lila Rose.

"Lila Rose," Alyssa would say, over and over. "This is Alyssa Reed and Lila Rose Reed," people would say, as if the sisters were married.

*   *   *

After the phone call, Alyssa followed her grandmother into the kitchen — knowing already, the way a person does when something bad has happened.

"What's up?" she asked.

Daisy G. opened the fridge and took out a pitcher of lemonade, pouring Alyssa a glass.

"I don't want lemonade," she said. "I want to know what happened."

Her grandmother was small and thin, with tiny hands and feet — fast-moving feet the size of a child's — and washed-out red frizzy hair that she dyed the color of Red Delicious apples. She had disappearing lips, painted large, twice their size, the color of plums. All her life, she had been a dancer, every kind of dancer. Even now, at seventy-seven, she'd put on tights and a leotard and tutu, and do her ballet exercises in front of the long mirror on Alyssa's bedroom door.

"No time to worry about the past, which is as dead as a doornail," she'd say to Alyssa, looking at herself in the mirror, pleased with what she saw, as if she were twenty, a great beauty with perfect dance form. "Just get on with today, and think about your plans tomorrow."

Alyssa put the lemonade back in the pitcher, the glass in the sink.

"So?"

"Stillborn," Daisy G. said, sinking into a chair at the kitchen table.

"'Stillborn'?"

"'Born dead,' is what we used to say," Daisy G. said, in that snappy way she had of telling the truth so it took the air out of a·person's lungs. "Which means she was already dead by the time she was born."

"What could have happened?" Alyssa asked quietly, picturing in her mind a doll and not a baby, born still with bendable arms and legs. Born dead.

"A terrible accident," Daisy G. looked at Alyssa from under the curtain of her green salamander eyes. "I will explain," she began, lifting her hands to illustrate her point. "There's a cord that attaches a baby to its mother. You know that."

"I know about that from science class," Alyssa said. "The umbilical cord."

"Well, that got twisted around the baby's neck, and she strangled before she had a chance to be born."

For a long time, they sat together at the table, with Daisy G. looking off into the middle distance. Not crying, although at any moment Alyssa expected that she would.

Fiona, the yellow tabby, walked across the table, back and forth between them, rubbing her soft fur against their arms, their cheeks.

"She had red hair like you," Daisy G. said, softly. "That's what your daddy told me."

"Freckles?"

"She was too young for freckles."

And then the telephone started to ring, one call after the next, and Daisy G. got up, rushed about the kitchen getting things out of the fridge, putting water on to boil, making coffee and oatmeal.

"Your father's coming home now, and you need some breakfast," she told Alyssa. "For strength."

"I'm not hungry," Alyssa said, slipping out the back door and away from the house. A sense of aimlessness was overtaking her, as if the day had deflated like a balloon empty of air. That's when she climbed the willow tree, halfway up, hidden by the weeping branches in full leaf, waiting.

Alyssa was ten years old. Ten ordinary years as an only child — although she had not known that her life had been so exquisitely happy until the morning when the baby died. She lived with her parents ten miles north of

North Haven, Connecticut, in an old farmhouse they rented from a banker. It stood at the end of a dirt road on six acres of land, with four cats — including Fiona — and some chickens belonging to the banker, and a goat whose job it was to mow the lawn with his teeth. Sometimes she walked to Norwood Elementary with her mother and father, walking in the middle between them, holding their hands. But by the time she was eight, she could walk home alone, crossing two streets, through the back gardens of the Everses, and the Stamans, and the Smiths, then across the Brownwells' pasture, where they used to keep cows. And home. At home, her mother — who had stopped working at the Art Barn Movie Theatre and Coffee Shop when Alyssa was born — would be baking cookies, or olive- or herb-bread, busying around the kitchen. Her grandmother would be sitting at the kitchen table dipping hot cookies in her coffee, listening to swing music on the radio.

"Do you think my life is perfect?" Alyssa had asked her grandmother one night in late October, after her tenth birthday party. That night, after the ice cream and cake, her father, out of the blue, had hopped into his pickup truck and not come home until dawn.

"No life is perfect, Alyssa," Daisy G. had said to her.

Her father owned a bowling alley in North Haven. On Saturdays, Alyssa could invite her friends from school over, and her father would allow them free sodas and hot dogs, and drive them in the back of his pickup truck. That is what happened on her tenth birthday. Except that on that Saturday, for the first time Alyssa could remember, her mother didn't come along to ride in the back with the kids and sit on the end seat of the first alley, her legs drawn up under her chin, watching them bowl.

"I've got to make supper and the birthday cake," was what she said. But later, Alyssa knew it was a half-truth. The chocolate fudge cake with yellow roses had been made already by Daisy G. and was sitting under a glass dome on top of the fridge.

The truck ride to North Haven was the best part: sitting on the ripply, hard, metal flatbed of the truck, with the wind blowing the tops of their heads so hard that their hair flew up like so many flags, as they giggled and held on to each other. It was too noisy in the back of the truck to talk.

This Saturday, the first alley was decorated with balloons, each printed with Alyssa's name, and there were ten party bags, one for each of her friends — full of tiny stuffed animals, stickers, candy corn, baby pumpkins, a fancy black mask with feathers, and lavender sparkles for their cheeks. But somehow Alyssa was uneasy, as if something were going on: a feeling in the air like a storm coming, although her friends were no different than they ever were, except for the added excitement that it was Alyssa's birthday and the extra giggles and showing off that went with the day.

Later, in the back of the truck, the sun going down, their hoods up against the cold wind, huddled together, their arms around one another, Alyssa remembered that all during the afternoon, her father had been gone. No one had chaperoned, except Eddie who worked the lanes — and probably Martin, her father's partner, had been watching off and on from the office.

"Where were you at my birthday party?" Alyssa asked her father on Sunday morning. Her mother sat in the rocker beside the radiator, looking out the window into the middle distance.

"Yes, Jack," Mary Reed had said sharply. "And last night? You missed the family party and the cake."

Her father's voice had a practiced calm about it. "I'd thought you were going to be at the party, Mary, and so I had a business lunch."

"A business lunch on Saturday?" she'd asked.

"He couldn't meet another time," her father had said. "Alyssa's friends were fine. The alley is practically a second home to them."

"I see," her mother had said, getting up from the rocker. "And last night?"

As she passed by on her way out of the kitchen, Alyssa could tell that she was crying.

Daisy G. told Alyssa that her mother was pregnant one afternoon in early January, snow accumulating on the ground, on their hair and faces, as they walked hand in hand with a roasting chicken and ice cream from the market.

"Don't say a word when they tell you," Daisy G. warned. "Your mother would kill me for telling you first."

Alyssa promised. "I've always wanted a baby," she said, a feeling of pure joy rushing through her blood.

"And it's a good thing too," Daisy G. said. "Maybe with a new baby on the way, your father will be home for dinner more often."

Alyssa had certainly noticed that her father came home late, sometimes after she was sleeping, even if her mother hadn't mentioned it. It used to be that her father came home just before dinner and they'd talk, sitting in the living room, his feet on the coffee table, the morning paper on his lap, Alyssa cross-legged on the floor, with a sleeping Fiona.

"I suppose he hopes the baby will be a boy," Alyssa said to Daisy G. — thinking, as she had for months, that perhaps her father had grown bored of conversations with her.

"I don't know what he had hoped because he never mentioned it," Daisy G. replied. "But they've done the tests, and the baby's a girl. She's going to be born in June."

"Mama will be very happy," Alyssa said, thinking of her mother lately, just in the past year, on the afternoons when Alyssa arrived from Norwood Elementary to find Mary Reed on the rocker in the kitchen, just staring out the window, the energy gone out of her.

"She is very happy," Daisy G. said. "And so is your father. They're almost back to the way it was when your mother was pregnant with you."

"How was it then?" Alyssa asked.

"They were ecstatic," Daisy G. said. "Delirious with happiness."

And Alyssa was pleased to think she had been responsible for such great happiness.

After the news of the baby, the winter of Alyssa's tenth year was nearly perfect. At least some of the time, her father came home early, as he used to do. Her mother was busy in the kitchen — cooking, or making bread and cookies — or fussing around the house, polishing, cleaning, or knitting little sweaters, or sewing curtains for the baby's room. Sometimes Alyssa even saw her parents kissing beside the kitchen sink. And then she'd hold her breath and tiptoe by the door, hoping by silence to capture the moment and not break the spell.

From her perch in the tree, she could see the kitchen through the large glass window. Her father was sitting at the table, his head in his hands. Daisy G. rushed around with dishes and the coffeepot; Fiona was curled up in the middle of the table next to a vase of purple lilacs. She could see her parents' bedroom, which faced the front of the house — and next to it, the baby's room.

Her mother had fixed up the room for the baby in the spring. She had painted it yellow and pasted a border of lambs and chickens around the ceiling, made white starchy curtains for the windows, brought out Alyssa's old bassinet and cleaned it up. There was a rocking chair and a Mother Goose rug and a patchwork quilt for the bassinet.

It occurred to Alyssa, seeing her father too sad to lift his head, that she should undo the baby's room. Take out the bassinet. Take down the curtains. Tear off the border of chickens and lambs. Hide the patchwork quilt. This had been her mother's workroom before, with a sewing machine and ironing board and small desk, all stored now in the attic. She could return the room to its former life, as if nothing had happened at all. Certainly a baby's room without a baby would break her mother's heart.

Alyssa stayed in the tree most of the morning, waiting for someone to notice that she was missing, to wonder where she had gone. It wasn't until the sun was nearly overhead that her father came out onto the porch and called her, his hands in his pockets, facing in the direction of the willow tree. Alyssa didn't answer. She watched him step down from the porch, cross the yard, and stand under the tree.

"Alyssa?" He looked up and saw her.

"Why didn't you call me earlier?" she asked. "I've been here for ten years, and you didn't even care."

"I knew where you were, sweetheart," he said, reaching up to help her down, hugging her hard as he lifted her to the ground.

"How's Mama?"

"Very sad," Jack Reed said.

"Me too." Alyssa took her father's hand, walking with him to the truck. He looked weary and sad, older than he had the day before. "I'm headed to the hospital," he said, kissing her good-bye.

"When will she be home?" she asked.

"Tonight, before dinner," he said, turning on the engine. "She wants to come home to us."

Daisy G. went to the grocery store after lunch.

"Lamb chops, mint jelly, potatoes, asparagus, and cherry pie," she read out the grocery list to Alyssa. "Your mama's favorite foods. I'll get some chocolate mints, and heavy cream for the pie, and some cat food for Fiona. You stay here and take care of the animals, and answer the phone."

And then she was gone, out the door, driving down the road in her old Toyota, barely able to see over the steering wheel.

Alyssa tore off the border of lambs and chickens first, standing on the small stepladder from the kitchen. The border came off easily, leaving only an occasional piece of wallpaper on the yellow wall. The bassinet was light, a basket on top of legs, and she carried it up to the attic, where she folded the little quilt — covering it with plastic to keep it clean, in case someday there would be another baby. She got the sewing machine in the attic down to the room, put up the ironing board and the iron the way they used to be. Then she took up the rug with Mother Goose in blue and yellow and put it in the attic, and she carried down the old straw mat that her mother used to keep in her workroom. When she was finished, it looked almost exactly the same as it had before the baby was expected to live there — except for the starchy curtains, which she left hanging, and the new yellow paint.

She hardly recognized her mother when she arrived with her father in the old truck. Not that Mary Reed had changed in looks exactly, although her eyes were black and pouchy and her belly was smaller than it had been, but still puffy. But *she* was different. She seemed suddenly very old and washed out — as if the person bathed in moonlight whom Alyssa had watched get into the truck in the middle of the night before was . . . gone. She smiled faintly at Alyssa, gave her a weak kiss, hardly even a kiss, on the top of her head, and collapsed in a chair at the kitchen table. Daisy G. bustled around the room bringing her tea and cookies, putting the cherry pie into the oven, salting the lamb chops, cutting up potatoes, and singing "la-la-la-la-la," since the radio wasn't playing her swing music.

"Please, Mama," Alyssa's mother said wearily. "Don't sing."

"Sorry, Mary. Sorry," Daisy G. said, reaching her arms around her daughter's shoulders. "Just trying for joy in sadness. For Alyssa's sake."

"For my sake, don't dance either," Mary Reed said.

"Certainly no dancing," Daisy G. agreed.

Alyssa slipped into the chair beside her mother.

"Would you tell me everything?" she asked quietly. Alyssa had been thinking about the baby, what she had looked like, what the doctor had said, whether it had been his fault. She wanted to be able to *see* what had happened as if she had been there. Particularly she wanted to know if this slip of a baby — once here and now gone — had looked exactly like her. And whether there would be a funeral.

"Your mother doesn't want to talk, sweetheart," Jack Reed said. "She's had a very hard day."

"I know." Alyssa leaned against her mother's shoulder.

But Mary Reed didn't lift her hands from her lap, didn't put her arm around Alyssa's shoulder, didn't even speak.

"There will be a funeral," Daisy G. said after dinner, while she and Alyssa were cleaning up — her parents in the living room, the living room silent. "Tomorrow, at Our Mother of Mercies."

"And will she be buried?"

"She will. In the graveyard beside the church."

"Even though she wasn't born alive."

"That's right," Daisy G. said. "But she was alive for a long time, waiting to be born."

"And will I be allowed to go?" Alyssa asked.

"You'll have to speak to your father about that," Daisy G. said, putting away the pie. "The pie wasn't very good, was it? Sort of like leather."

"Not exactly delicious," Alyssa agreed, looking in the living room. She was hoping to ask her parents about the funeral.

But her mother had gotten up, dragging a sweater behind her, and was headed slowly up the stairs, her head down, her shoulders curled under the weight of trouble.

It was dusk, not yet quite dark, but Alyssa had left the light on in the former baby's room, imagining that when Mary Reed got to the top of the steps, she would look to the right — and there would be her old workroom, practically the way it used to be. Unless, of course, her mother looked straight ahead into the bedroom she shared with Alyssa's father, walked across the room and fell on her bed in misery — then she might miss seeing what Alyssa had done for her.

Later, Alyssa tried to remember what she had expected to happen when her mother saw the baby's room changed back to the workroom. Pleasure is what she had expected. Gratitude.

Certainly not what happened. Not the long, terrible scream that pierced the silence of the house.

"I was trying to make it better for Mama," Alyssa said to her father, much later, when he came into her room to tell her good night. "I wanted to make her not so sad."

"I understand what you were doing, Alyssa — but unfortunately, it didn't work," her father said, kissing her absently, turning off the lamp.

Alyssa lay quietly in her bed, the covers pulled up under her chin, her face turned to the window, the light from a full moon washing her face silver. She didn't move, hoping to sleep soon, hoping for the night to be over, for the sun to wake her to a new day. Then she heard the tiny footsteps of Daisy G. in her high heels rushing up the stairs, clicking across the wooden floor into the guest room.

Alyssa got out of bed and walked down the hall, then knocked on the closed door. She whispered, "Daisy G.? Are you awake?"

"Of course, of course," her grandmother replied, opening the door. "Come in, sit down on the bed. I'm wide-awake. I won't sleep for days now."

"I feel terrible," Alyssa said.

Daisy G. sat down on the bed beside her.

"Don't worry," she said. "Your heart was in the right place."

"I didn't want her to see the room all fixed up for a baby."

"Of course you didn't," Daisy G. said.

"Are things going to be all right?" Alyssa asked, feeling desperate. "Do you think they will?"

"Pretty soon. Not soon enough, but before very long, things will be back to the way they used to be."

"You promise me?"

"I can't make promises like that. I can only hope, but I don't know the answer to the future — my sweet, my angel, my small and perfect tangerine."

"I don't think things will be back the way they used to be," Alyssa said. "I don't think they'll ever be the same again."

CHAPTER TWO

In the first week after the baby died, everyone was at home. Daisy G. cooked and baked: mainly delicate sweets — tiny cookies, ginger cake with whipped cream, and something she called "Strawberry Surprise," which was red, and thick, and too sugary to swallow without choking. Alyssa's father planted a small garden, with rows of vegetables and annuals and herbs, something to keep her mother busy during the long summer days — "to keep her mind off the baby," is what he told Alyssa. Her mother sat on the porch swing, barefooted, wearing one of her husband's button-down shirts with the sleeves rolled up. She kept a straw hat pulled down on her forehead as protection against the sun, although the swing was in the shadows.

Alyssa hung around — sometimes working in the kitchen with her grandmother, or leaning against the porch pillars and keeping her mother company, or digging in the garden with her father — playing with the cats and the goat, and thinking about the perfectly formed Lila Rose, whose image she couldn't erase from her mind.

"I'm going back to work next week, Alyssa," her father told her, late on Friday afternoon. "And Daisy G. has to go back home and be about her own life. So it'll be just you and Mama."

"That's okay," Alyssa said. "That's just fine. A lot of times it was just me and Mama, before the baby died."

Her father was on his hands and knees, putting in the tiny kale and spinach plants he had bought at the nursery, since it was too late in the season to plant from seed.

"That's true," he said. "But now the baby's gone." He sat up on his haunches and looked without smiling at Alyssa. "In your mama's mind, there's more gone than the baby."

"What does that mean?" Alyssa asked, crouching next to him, digging a hole for a tomato plant that was still sitting in a flat.

"It means she's going to have a hard time rallying."

"What do you think he meant by 'rallying'?" she asked Daisy G. later in the evening, when they were doing the dishes together. Her parents were upstairs, the soft rumble of their conversation rolling down the stairwell.

Daisy G. shook her head.

"And what more is gone besides the baby?" she asked, sitting on a stool beside her grandmother.

Daisy G. wiped the dishwater off her hands and leaned against the kitchen sink.

"Your parents had a lot of hope about that baby," she said. "Remember? I said that when I told you about the baby."

"Hope for what? A boy? You never told me what kind of baby they wanted. I suppose they could have wanted a boy, but they never said so. They just said they wanted a baby, and I thought they'd be happy with whatever kind of baby they got."

"They hoped for a brand-new baby. That's all." She

stuck her finger in the middle of the leftover Strawberry Surprise and licked it. "Sometimes they fought, you know."

"Everybody fights in families," Alyssa said. "That's what my friends say. Everybody, including their parents."

Her grandmother wrapped the remaining chicken from dinner in silver foil, then covered the dishes of peas and potatos and corn.

"I talked to my friend Amy, and she says her parents fight all the time and they love each other anyway and once her father even threw his dinner at her mother."

Daisy G. shrugged. "This is not a conversation that has a future, Alyssa. Let's talk about something else."

"But I want to know — do you think my parents fight more than other people?" Alyssa asked.

"Who knows about other people, sweet potato? I don't know any secrets about people, including your parents. I just know they hoped that a new baby would help them stop fighting."

"That's a funny thing to hope," Alyssa said.

"People are like that," Daisy G. said. "Very funny in their hoping."

After Alyssa's father went back to work, her mother got worse. She'd sit in the rocker, with her feet together just so, her arms at her sides, her hands loose as a rag doll's, and rock. The creaking back and forth in the empty house drove Alyssa crazy. Some days she'd flop down on her bed and put a pillow over her head to drown out the *click-clock, click-clock* steady on the linoleum floor.

"You ought to go see your friends, sweet pea," Daisy G. said, as she was baking muffins for breakfast. She came over every afternoon to make dinner in the evening, late after the sun had gone down, while they waited for Alyssa's father, who had a lot of work at the bowling alley. Sometimes he didn't get home until after midnight.

Alyssa shrugged. She was lying on the floor on her back, her legs propped up on the wall, watching the cherry Popsicle she was eating melt, dripping red polka dots on her shirt.

"I don't want to see my friends now," Alyssa said.

Daisy G. licked the batter spoon, then put the muffins in the oven.

"And why would that be? You have seven good friends. You told me that last fall."

"Pretty good friends," Alyssa said. "Maybe five of them."

"It would be good for you to get out of this gloomy house and spend some time with them."

"Maybe," she said, closing her eyes, letting the cherry juice drip on the lids. "But sometimes, when there's trouble, you don't want to see anybody."

Her friends had called. Three of them — Sally Jewel, Mara Staples, and Randy Sue Field — called when they heard about the baby. But Alyssa discovered that she couldn't talk to them the way she used to, just weeks ago, as if what had happened had caused a wall to go up between them, as if they'd changed and weren't exactly the same friends they'd been.

"Trouble can make some people uneasy," Daisy G. said. "They worry it could be catching."

"But I'm still the same girl I was," she said.

"Almost," Daisy G. said, "but not exactly."

At the end of June, Alyssa's father went on a business trip.

"What kind of business trip?" Alyssa was lying across the bottom of her parents' bed with Fiona.

"To look at other bowling alleys, for remodeling ideas," he said, packing up his suitcase.

"You've never traveled before."

"We're making the bowling alley bigger, so we need to

look at other ones," he said. "It's perfectly normal. Fathers go on business trips."

Her mother was sitting up in bed in the lilac cotton skirt she'd been wearing for days, and a blue button-down shirt. Her hair was tied back in a ponytail, her arm flung across her eyes.

"You could have chosen a better time to leave, Jack," she said, her voice muffled by sadness.

Jack Reed moved Alyssa's legs and sat down.

"I waited until you felt better, Mary, and then I had to take this trip. Two days. That's all the time I'll be gone."

"We'll be fine, Mama," Alyssa said. "Maybe we'll drive to town and go shopping. Or go to the movies, or out to dinner. Something fun."

Mary Reed didn't reply.

"Daisy G. wanted us to go to New York for the weekend, to see a dance program."

"I don't want to go to New York," her mother said.

They didn't go to New York. They didn't go shopping, or to the movies, or out to dinner.

The night after Jack Reed left on his business trip, a summer rain blew against the screens. It was especially dark that night, with a kind of hollowness in the atmosphere — as if the Reeds' house were a cave deep in the center of a black mountain, and they were trapped inside. With Daisy G. at the grocery store, and only Alyssa and the cats at home, Mary Reed began to weep.

She was sitting on the couch in the living room, sewing buttons on Jack Reed's dress shirts, when it started.

Alyssa was talking on the telephone to Sally Jewel, but she heard the crying and ran downstairs. By the time she got to the living room, her mother was sobbing — great loud wails — her shoulders shaking so hard it seemed she might break in two.

"Mama," Alyssa said, as she got down on her knees beside the couch. "What's happened to you?"

But her mother couldn't speak. She couldn't catch her breath.

Mr. Aiken, the man who answered the telephone at the grocery store, said that Yes, he'd seen Daisy G. — she was standing in dairy products with her grocery cart — and he'd get her to come to the phone, which he did.

Alyssa helped her grandmother put Mary Reed — still weeping, but softly — in the back of Daisy G.'s car, and they drove a very long way through the night to a hospital in New Haven. Her mother stayed there for two weeks, and no one could go see her or talk to her on the telephone.

"Hospital rules," Daisy G. said.

She called what had happened to Alyssa's mother a "breakdown."

"Heartsick from sadness," was what Alyssa told her friends from school, and the lady at the pharmacy, and Mr. Aiken at the grocery store.

At home, Alyssa worked. She helped Daisy G. with dinner, and learned how to roast a chicken, and make tomato sauce for pasta, and bake a chocolate cake with vanilla icing and sprinkles. She worked in the garden, weeding and watering, and fed the cats and the goats. She scrubbed the kitchen floor, and cleaned out the fridge and her closet, and straightened the attic. Working as she did, without stopping, kept her from thinking about her childhood shattered by Lila Rose's death.

"It wasn't perfect, banana cake," Daisy G. said, stirring tomato soup, slicing cheddar cheese for grilling sandwiches. "You are forgetting. There was a low boil of trouble all the time."

"Whatever," Alyssa said. Although she knew, of

course — knew the low hum of danger in the house, especially in the months before the baby. But it wasn't the way she wanted to remember her life. "Perfect is what I remember. I never knew about the trouble."

"You know what you want to know," Daisy G. said, turning up the swing music on the radio, grabbing Alyssa by the hand and swirling her across the kitchen floor.

CHAPTER THREE

The week before the beginning of school, the Reeds moved to an apartment in North Haven near the bowling alley. The apartment was small and new, and smelled of cleaning fluid and mothballs and carpet cleaner. There were two small bedrooms, with a view over the parking lot, and the building had restrictions. No cats allowed. No chickens, certainly. No goats.

"Why do we have to move?" Alyssa asked.

"We just do." Jack Reed threw up his hands. "Your mother," he said.

"I can take care of Mama," Alyssa said.

"Not when you start school in the fall."

"Then Daisy G. can be here, while I'm at school."

"Daisy G. is busy," Jack said. "She has her own life. We can't ask her to take care of us."

"Like what does she have to do? Dancing?"

"She has lots of things to do. And already she spends a lot of time with your mother."

All summer, after she got out of the hospital, Mary Reed lay around, on the couch in the living room, on the chaise in the backyard, or in a rocking chair in the kitchen, staring out the window at a craggy apple tree full of small hard green apples. Sometimes she didn't even get out of bed.

The decision to move was actually made while Mary Reed was in the hospital, but no one told Alyssa's mother until later.

"So she doesn't even have a chance to say no?" Alyssa asked one night at dinner.

"Your mother and I talked about moving into the city before she got sick, Alyssa," her father said. "She wanted to move. She needed more to do, with you in school all day and the baby gone. She thought she might look for a job."

He had already found the apartment and paid his money down and taken Daisy G. to North Haven to see it.

"What about you?" Alyssa asked Daisy G. "You'll move with us, won't you?"

"I think I'll stay here in my own apartment," Daisy G. said. "I have my routines."

"What if we need you?"

Daisy G. closed her eyes, put her head back so she faced the ceiling, shaking her head.

"If you need me, I'll be there lickety-split — on a dime, pronto," Daisy G. said.

So they moved the week before school: Daisy G. packed up, her father loaded the back of the truck, and then unloaded everything at the new apartment. Mary Reed was too tired to help.

"What's the matter with her now?" Alyssa asked. "I thought the hospital would fix her."

"Sadness," Daisy G. said. "Just like you thought. Hospitals don't fix sadness."

"You're twice as old as she is and you're never tired,"

Alyssa said to Daisy G., who was carrying dining-room chairs up the two sets of stairs to the second-floor apartment.

"Luck of the draw, sweetheart," Daisy G. said. "We're made of elastic, you and me. Knock us down and we pop right up."

"What about Mama?"

"No elastic that I've ever seen."

"But at least she used to be happy," Alyssa said, putting the chairs around the dining-room table.

"You've got to be able to be happy when things are bad, as well as when things are good. And your mama can't seem to do that."

The first night in the apartment, as Alyssa marked in the five-year diary she'd gotten from Daisy G. on her tenth birthday, her father stayed out until midnight. He had been at the apartment all day — carrying in the furniture, making the beds, arranging the furniture the way Mary Reed asked him to arrange it, directing him from the couch where she was lying. He'd gone to the grocery store and picked up staples, enough food for the next day: fruit, milk, orange juice, bread, cereal, tomatoes, and cheese. Then he'd gone away — to the bowling alley, he'd said.

But later, when Alyssa called the bowling alley, he wasn't there.

By nine o'clock, when the darkness of late summer had settled around the apartment complex in North Haven, Mary Reed climbed into bed with a headache, and Alyssa paced — up and down the living room, into her room and out — then she stood in the doorway surveying the room where she would be living her new life. The yellow buttercup quilt, the brown straw rug, the rocking chair, and the pinewood dresser were there. The bookcase with her favorite books and the baby picture of her with her parents framed on the dresser, and the photograph of the cats: Fiona sleeping on the same table that was now in the dining room of the new apartment, and the collection of antique cat prints that Daisy G. had given her after a trip to New York City — they all seemed out of place in this new room, with its blond wood floor and metal-framed windows, smelling of cleaning fluid. Alyssa looked in on her mother, who was already sleeping, and called the bowling alley again.

Martin, her father's partner, answered the phone. "Jack isn't here, Alyssa. He hasn't come back."

"Are you expecting him soon?" Alyssa asked.

"We close at ten o'clock," he said. "I don't think so."

* * *

Alyssa waited. She sat on the couch with her feet on the coffee table, her arms folded across her chest. She was half-worried that her father might have been in some kind of accident, half-furious at him for not being at home.

When he did come in, shortly after midnight, he walked so quietly up the stairs of the building that Alyssa hardly heard him until the key turned in the lock. He was irritated.

"What are you doing up after midnight, Alyssa?" he asked, walking into the kitchen and opening the fridge.

"What are *you* doing home so late, on our first night in this dump you've made us move to?"

Jack Reed closed the refrigerator door, walked into the living room, and leaned against the wing chair opposite the couch.

"It isn't a dump," he said. "You'll learn to like it."

"I didn't want to move," Alyssa said.

"That's a different thing."

He sat down in the chair and put his feet on the coffee table by Alyssa's.

"I don't like change," she told him.

"No one does."

"But I'm a child, and I don't have any control over what happens to me."

"None of us really has control."

"Wrong," Alyssa said. "You decide we move, and so we move. That's control, and I don't have it."

Her father sat across from her, his arms crossed, his hair disheveled, and his eyes half closed, as if he didn't want to see too much around him.

"So?"

Her father tucked his shirt in, folded his hands together, sat up straighter on the chair, and leaned forward. She could tell he was about to say something that she didn't want to hear. There was something in his attitude, the formality of his folded hands, the flatness of his lips, the way he sighed — as if he were getting rid of all the air in his lungs before he spoke.

"Like, what now?" she asked.

She wanted to get up from the couch, take her father's keys to the truck, open the door to the apartment, run down the steps, out the door, and along the path to the parking lot where the truck was parked, then hop in the cab and drive away. Daisy G.'s is where she'd go, straight out of town: north of North Haven on Route 95, past three exits until she got to Meadowville, Connecticut, and the house where she used to live, to Daisy G.'s apartment in the building in back of the grocery store, by the lake.

"I am unhappy," Jack Reed was saying.

"You're unhappy?" Alyssa asked. "How do you think I feel? You're at work all day and I'm here by myself or with Daisy G., and Mama's sleeping or sitting looking at nothing at all."

"I know it's hard for you, Alyssa, but for me, it's been killing."

"What do you mean *killing*?"

"I mean it's too difficult for me to live this way is what I mean. That's it — pure and simple," her father said.

She knew that voice and what it meant very well. Whenever she heard it, there was a problem on its way. Some dissatisfaction or anger or disappointment or bad temper her father was getting ready to express.

And that's exactly what happened.

"I'm moving to another apartment," Jack Reed said.

For a while — weeks maybe, maybe even months — he was going to move to another apartment.

"I have to leave," he told her.

"You have to leave what?"

"Just leave this apartment, with you and Mama —

briefly, for a short time — until things get better with your mother."

"I see. Leave. L-e-a-v-e," she spelled it out. "Fine. Do whatever you wish. That's perfectly fine with me." Alyssa was pleased with the crackle of ice in her voice. "Go, then. It's a free world." She got up from the couch. "I think I'll go too. I plan to rent an apartment — take my stuff out of my room and buy some furniture on your credit card and move — and you won't even know my telephone number."

She went into her room and shut the door, pulling the little silver lock just in case her father decided he wanted to come in.

"Don't bother to knock," she called beyond the wooden door.

Facedown on the bed, her arms tight against her sides, her stomach fluttering, her cheeks hot with rage, Alyssa made a decision. The world as she had known it was gone. "Kaput," as Daisy G. would say. And this new world, this apartment with its white, white walls and lonely views of parking lots and the smell of other people's cooking — with her father leaving and her mother disappearing into herself — this was not a good place for her to be.

Since she couldn't depend on her mother and father,

who had turned out to be made of breakable glass, then she'd depend on herself. After all, she was "elastic," just as Daisy G. had told her.

When she opened the door to her bedroom to go get a glass of milk, her father was still sitting in the living room. He was staring out into the darkness.

"Alyssa?" he began.

" 'Blister,' " she said. "Like when your shoes are too tight."

" 'Blister'?"

"That's my new name," she said, turning the corner into the kitchen. "I've dropped 'Alyssa Reed' forever."

CHAPTER FOUR

Alyssa Reed?"

Ms. Covington, the Section A fifth-grade teacher, leaned against the blackboard, a pencil behind her ear. It was the first day of school at Bixley Elementary.

"Blister," said Blister, formerly Alyssa Reed. She sat in the front row, her back straight, her frizzy red hair in a high ponytail, some blush for a look of good health on her pale freckled cheeks, like she had seen in the September *Seventeen*.

"'Blister'?" Ms. Covington had a way about her. She was young, with a ponytail herself, wearing tight black pants, and small, not much taller than some of the fifth-grade boys. "'Blister' must be your nickname. Blister Reed."

"My real name. Just Blister. Drop the 'Reed.'"

She didn't turn around, but she could hear giggling in the back of the room behind her desk, the high-pitched voices of girls.

"Welcome to Bixley Elementary," Ms. Covington said. "I think you're the only new girl in the fifth grade this year. Right, class?"

"Riiiiight" chorused around the room.

"So tell us about yourself."

Blister had planned this moment, had decided what she would say about her past if she happened to be asked. How much she would tell, how much she would make up — to protect her mother, who had still been sleeping when Blister had left the apartment that morning. What she would say about her father who had moved to a new place in late August. And especially, what she would say about herself.

She stood up very straight, her arms folded across her chest, her head cocked. Her voice was strong.

"Not much has happened in my life," she began. "I

used to live in Meadowville on a chicken farm, with goats and cats and four horses; and then my little sister Lila Rose died, and my father wanted to move out of the house where we'd all lived together, and now I'm here."

"A lot has happened to you," Ms. Covington said, in one of those soft, sympathetic voices.

The class was silent. Blister could feel people's attention, their sudden interest in her — Blister, formerly Alyssa Reed — a stranger acquainted with a sadness unfamiliar to most ten year olds.

"Thank you," she said quietly.

When the bell rang for recess, some girls gathered around her in a rush, pressing in as she put her backpack over her shoulder. They told her to follow them to the playground; they wanted to talk.

One girl called Anne — tall and skinny, with a single blond braid down to the middle of her back, and black high-tops — walked arm in arm with Blister out of the classroom.

"What happened to the horses and stuff when you moved?" she asked.

"We gave them away," Blister said. "We had to, because we moved to an apartment."

"How perfectly terrible!" cried a small, dark girl with an accent, who introduced herself to Blister as Veronique.

"And what happened to your sister?" Anne asked.

"She just died," Blister said.

"Like that?" Anne asked. "I didn't know children just died, without a sickness."

"Sometimes they do." Blister shrugged. "Lila Rose did. She had red hair like me."

"How old was she?" another girl asked.

Blister considered. She hadn't thought they would ask particular questions. But "Born dead" didn't seem to be an answer equal to the situation she had created, and to say that Lila Rose was a baby when she died seemed wrong as well.

"Little," she said.

"Little" seemed to cover every possibility: a sweet, sad word that suited the occasion.

Veronique took a package of M&M's out of her pocket and passed them around, looping her arm around Blister's shoulder.

"So now you're an only child?"

Blister nodded.

"I'm an only child too," she said. "Me and Bylynda."

Bylynda was leaning against the jungle gym — she had

short, black, curly hair and glittery dark eyes — a big girl with a kind of attitude. Blister could tell by the way she stood, and the way the other girls responded to her, that Bylynda was a girl of consequence at Bixley Elementary.

"Bylynda was new last year," Veronique said. "She moved from Texas because her parents got divorced. Right, Bylynda?"

"Right. My mom and me and our parrot, Constantine," she said breezily. "My father's a nightmare. We call him Pat, the Rat."

"That's really too bad," Blister said, sticking her hands in her pockets as she had noticed Bylynda doing, leaning against the jungle gym next to her.

"No, it's not," Bylynda said. "It's a godsend, my mom says."

At her old school in Meadowville, Blister hadn't known anyone whose parents were divorced. Everyone there had two parents, except for Billy Taylor, whose father was dead, and Mara Huggins, whose mother had been sick in the hospital all of fourth grade. She was pleased to meet someone whose life might be similar to her own. That is, if her father actually didn't come back to the place where Blister and her mother lived, as he had promised to do.

"My father lives in Houston with his new witch wife.

Mom says we're lucky to be done with him," Bylynda said, waving to a group of girls across the blacktop. "See those girls, Blister?"

Blister nodded. Several girls were walking across the blacktop in short-short skirts and tiny T-shirts, their arms around each other, their matching ponytails bouncing.

"Those are the cheerleaders. They're the most popular girls in the school."

"Ten cheerleaders: five from the sixth grade, and five from the fifth," Anne said, her voice hushed. "Me and Veronique and Bylynda and some of the other girls in the class are trying out for this year's squad — but it's, like, impossible to be chosen."

"Unless you're very popular," Bylynda said.

"Right," Anne agreed. "Popularity is the most important part."

But at the moment, Blister wasn't listening. The conversation about cheerleading slipped over her. She was thinking about Bylynda's father and his witch wife. Suddenly it struck her that her father, like Bylynda's, could have an entirely new life without her, the former Alyssa Reed. Although she had believed what he had told her — believed that soon, maybe by Christmas, he'd move back to the apartment — who could say? Perhaps he had other plans already.

She followed the girls back into the classroom and took a seat at her desk for social studies period.

It was possible, she supposed, that he might not come home again — ever. No one could make him.

Blister headed home from school alone. She had hoped for company, for one of the girls she had talked to on the playground, who might live nearby to meet up with her. Maybe they'd begin to be friends, and walk back and forth to school together. But as she was leaving the front door of the building, she saw the pack of them — Anne, Bylynda, Veronique, and a couple of others — standing on the front steps huddled together, laughing and talking. She guessed that they were probably making their plans to practice for cheerleading tryouts. Maybe, she thought, she'd walk by them — wave hello in a breezy way, then call, "See you later," or "See you tomorrow," as if she hadn't a care in the world. But locked together as they were, they didn't look particularly friendly. So she headed down the steps another way and went home, without looking back.

*   *   *

At the drugstore where Blister stopped to buy candy for her mother — Hershey's Kisses, which her father used to bring home to her mother from the bowling alley — a girl she recognized from her class was standing in line to buy magazines. Blister had noticed her on the way to school in the morning. She'd been walking just ahead, her shoulders slumped, her book bag dragging behind, her pale hair long and scrambled. Then she had seen the same girl at the back of the class, in the last seat in the far corner, with a sour expression on her small, white face.

"Hi," Blister said.

"I know who you are. I heard what you said today about your sister." The girl paid for her magazines.

"I saw you too."

"You probably don't know me. I'm Sara Barton."

"I'm Blister."

"I know," Sara said. "It's sort of a weird name."

"I made it up since I was coming to a new school."

"I probably should tell you that you're going to hate Bixley." Sara folded her arms across her chest.

"How come?"

"Just because." Sara shrugged. "The girls, especially. I've been here since kindergarten, and the girls have gotten worse every year."

"Which girls?"

"All the girls are catastrophes, unless you turn out to be popular."

Blister paid the cashier and stuffed the chocolate kisses in her pocket.

"Well, I probably won't turn out to be popular," she said, walking out of the drugstore with Sara.

"Probably not," Sara said. "I'm certainly not. I was only invited to one birthday party last year, and that's because everybody in the world was invited to Veronique's birthday party — and no one asked me to sleep over."

"You can spend the night at my house this year, if you want," Blister said. "Once we get it sort of fixed up."

"My mother says the reason the girls are awful is because in some schools there are cliques, and Bixley is one of them."

"In my old school, everyone liked each other," Blister said.

"You were lucky. But then, you've never been in fifth grade before. My mother says that fifth grade is particularly awful, because girls turn suddenly mean." She stopped at the light. "I live there." She pointed to a brick house with two large pine trees on either side of the front door. "It's a duplex."

And then after delivering her bad news, Sara Barton crossed the street, without saying good-bye.

Daisy G. was in the apartment when Blister arrived. She could tell from the music, even before she opened the apartment door. There was Daisy G., in black tights and a sweatshirt with "Love Me Tender" written in white letters. She'd put on her ballet shoes and was doing little leaps across the bare apartment floor.

For a change, her mother wasn't on the couch.

"Alyssa, my sweet — thank goodness you're home! I was worried."

She wrapped her arms around Blister's shoulders, kissed her all over the top of her head. Sometimes she was like that, a regular grandmother. And sometimes, as Mary Reed said to Blister on several occasions, she was brittle and sharp-tongued. "She's always been like that," Blister's mother had said. "Even when I was young. Harder on me because I'm her daughter, I suppose."

Daisy G. took Blister's hand and kissed her fingers. "So here we are, just you and me in this boring apartment. And we're going to turn it into a sunshine palace for your mama when she comes home."

"Where is Mama?" Blister asked.

"At the doctor," Daisy G. said, arranging pepper plants with tiny red peppers on the windowsill, filling a vase with water, stuffing daisies in the vase, and draping a bright yellow blanket on the couch. "Nobody could possibly live in this place without being depressed. No wonder your mama sleeps all day."

Blister peered into the paper bags full of the goodies that Daisy G. had brought — quilts, and pictures, and pillows, and a box of chocolates, and two lamps, and groceries for supper.

"We're making a home," Daisy G. said. "You and me, sweetheart. Nothing can stop us."

And so they did, transforming the apartment into a place that felt a little bit like the old house in Meadowville — except for the absence of the cats, who had stayed on at the farm because the apartment didn't allow pets.

Daisy G. cooked a beef stew, set the table for dinner, and put three red tulips in the middle of the table. Just before six o'clock, Mary Reed came home. She was smiling, for the first time since August.

"Did you meet anyone you liked at school today?" her mother asked her at dinner.

"Lots of girls," Blister said. She had been thinking about what Sara had told her, and about the closed circle of girls outside the school when she left that afternoon. But she certainly wasn't going to tell her mother that. "No boys, but I'll have plenty of friends here. Maybe I'll even try out for the cheerleading squad."

"Cheerleading — now, that's a good idea!" Daisy G. said. "Your mother was a cheerleader. She was the best cheerleader Springfield High School ever had. Captain, weren't you, Mary?"

"Yes," Blister's mother said. "I was captain."

"You never told me you'd been a cheerleader," Blister said.

"That was so long ago I can hardly remember."

It was late when they finished dinner, and raining, a heavy rain, with rolls of thunder in the distance. Daisy G. decided to spend the night.

"So, what do you hear from your father?" Daisy G. asked after Blister's mother had gone to bed.

"I'm supposed to have dinner with him once in the middle of the week, and spend every other weekend at his apartment. That's the arrangement."

"What kind of arrangement is that?"

"Well, we had to have plans, so sometimes I'm with Mama and sometimes with him."

"How many times have you seen him so far since he moved?" Daisy G. asked.

"He only moved two weeks ago, and I haven't seen him yet. But he called yesterday to wish me 'good luck' on my first day at the new school. I'll visit him soon."

"He should be punished, sent to his room without dinner," Daisy G. said.

"He's busy this fall, building an addition to the bowling alley, twelve new lanes and a game room."

"Well, I'm going to call him on the telephone."

"Don't do that, Daisy G. He's doing his best, and he might get mad."

"Not at me, he won't," Daisy G. said. She crawled under the covers with Blister and pulled up a light blanket.

Blister wriggled over next to her grandmother, lining her body up next to Daisy G.'s.

"I wish you could live with us."

"No you don't, sweetheart," she said. "I'd drive you crazy, with my music and rehearsal schedule."

"What are you rehearsing for?" Blister asked.

"I have a performance in October. Two weeks at Dance Place in New Haven. I have a lot of work to do."

"A real performance? You never told me."

Daisy G. giggled.

"Not exactly a real performance, sweetheart. But I have to have a plan, so I think of performances and pretend they're real."

"I'm a good pretender," Blister said.

"You're better than you think," Daisy G. said, sleepily. "You always need to have a plan."

Later, as she lay in bed, unable to sleep — with Daisy G. making little cat snores beside her — Blister thought of a plan.

She certainly wasn't going to sit around and wait for her mother to be happy again, or for her father to come home.

" 'No use trying to change the things you can't change,' " Daisy G. would say.

But with a little work, she could be a cheerleader. Maybe even captain.

CHAPTER FIVE

Blister stood in the window of her father's bedroom on the second floor of the Beechtree Garden Apartments in North Haven. It was a Saturday morning in early October — cool, brilliantly sunny, a perfect day to be outside. Her father had suggested that they rent bikes after breakfast and cycle along the towpath by the river — although he should have remembered that Blister had hated biking ever since the first grade, when she plowed her two-wheeler into Boogey Martin at the Halloween parade in Meadowville.

Shading her eyes from the sun's glitter, she watched her father walk out of the apartment building in his blue sweats, a baseball cap on backward, slouching, pretending to be eighteen instead of thirty-seven, which was the age he happened to be as of the day before yesterday. He was carrying a load of dirty laundry. She watched him open the door of his sky-blue Toyota, toss the laundry in the front seat, and drive off to the laundromat and the grocery store.

"Be back in an hour," he had said. "I'll just get some milk and cereal, and drop off the laundry. Want to come?"

"No, thanks," Blister replied. "I've got some stuff to do."

"What kind of stuff?"

"Just stuff," she said.

Which was perfectly true.

Underneath her father's double bed was a blue canvas suitcase that didn't belong to him. She had noticed it the night before, when she'd arrived to spend the weekend at the apartment her father had rented when he'd decided that life with Blister's mother was unbearable.

She waited at the window of her father's bedroom, just in case he suddenly remembered that he had forgotten something. He was always forgetting something: her tenth birthday; his wallet, when they went out to dinner at Maxie's Pizzeria; his promise to take her to New York City to see a play on Broadway; her uncle's telephone number. Big and little things he forgot.

"Your daddy's a dreamer," her mother used to say, before the baby died, before she went to the hospital, back when Mary Reed had loved Jack Reed with all her heart. "That's what people always say about him."

Blister checked the clock beside the bed. 7:45. That gave her almost an hour while her father was at the laundromat doing the wash, and then at the grocery store getting breakfast, and going back to the laundromat to change the clothes to the dryer. Enough time for her plans.

She pulled the blue canvas bag from under the bed and unzipped it, her heart beating for fear of the secrets she might discover inside the bag, her heart beating for her sins.

The first time Blister had visited the Beechtree apartments was in the middle of September — after her first week at Bixley Elementary — and she had been amazed. Her father's apartment was actually fixed up, a regular decorated place: with bedspreads, and rugs, and pictures on the wall, and flowers in a vase on the table in the living room, and new plates and knives and forks, and pots and pans, and soft olive-green towels in the bathroom — as if Jack Reed had suddenly gotten rich or domestic or both. It was astonishing how neat things were. When her father had lived with Mary Reed, he didn't even make the bed or wash the dishes or vacuum.

Since the middle of September, she had seen her father twice, two weekends — Friday after school through Sunday lunch. That was the arrangement. Except for the mid-week dinners, which hadn't happened yet. It was the only time she saw him unless there was an emergency, which so far there hadn't been. Although she had been thinking of inventing one — attention deficit disorder or depression, like her mother's. She had his telephone number, but the answering machine was always on, so she never got to talk to him immediately; and when she called the bowling alley, he was always someplace else. After school, she sat by the telephone at her own apartment waiting for him to return her call. Which sometimes he did, and sometimes he forgot.

"You shouldn't have left me with Mama," Blister had said, the first time she visited him at the new apartment. "I'm too much trouble for her."

"She needs you, sweetheart," her father said.

She loved the way he called her "sweetheart," like Daisy G., sort of round and soft, as if she were delicious. She loved the way he sometimes kissed the top of her head absentmindedly.

She wanted to say that her mother was too sad and weak and ill for a girl as young as Blister to count on.

"She's acting sick again, the way she did in the summer," she said to him.

"Don't let her do that to you," he had said. "She plays at being sick."

"But sometimes she doesn't even get out of bed, Daddy," she said, hearing the whine in her own voice, wishing to sound more convincing.

"Mary has a tendency to do that sort of thing, Alyssa, winding you into her web like a spider queen. You've got to be strong."

"I am strong," Blister said. "That's not the point at all. Daisy G. thinks Mama's in terrible shape, that she doesn't have the strength to live when bad things happen." She leaned against the door, her arms folded across her chest. "And a lot of bad things have happened lately. Some on purpose."

"I think you ought to pay attention to how your mother is with you."

"I do."

"You need to figure out the difference between her being sick, and manipulating you to think she's sick."

Blister thought about that later, about whether Mary Reed had been acting sick on purpose, perhaps to get Jack Reed to pay attention to her, or to move back home, or to buy her yellow roses the way he used to do when she was pregnant with Lila Rose. Alyssa didn't know enough about grown-ups, about whether they pretended to be sick when they weren't. But she did know her mother seemed miserable.

"It might be better if I lived with you," Blister said to her father. He was sitting on the couch, the newspaper on his lap, glancing at the headlines.

"I don't think that would work, Alyssa," he said.

"Why do you say that?" she asked, her voice breaking.

"I'm sorry, darling. I wish things could be different," he said, softly. "But, your mother *needs* you, especially now. I would never take you away from her at this moment."

"Great," she had said, getting up from the couch, feeling the tears rushing into her throat. "Thanks a lot. Let me know the next time you have good news." Then she rushed into her father's study and slammed the door.

Blister closed her eyes and pulled open the blue canvas bag.

Later, she couldn't remember what she had expected to find there. Something, or her heart wouldn't have been beating so hard. Something, or she wouldn't have spent last night planning to search the contents as soon as her father left her alone in the apartment. But what she did discover was more than she had expected or wished to find.

Underwear was at the top. Lots of it. More than a single person could possibly need. Tiny bikini panties in yellow and pale pink and powdery blue, with lace around the legs; see-through black silk bikinis and a matching bra stuffed to give the wearer large round breasts. A slip of a nightgown with thin straps, a garden of silk roses.

She went into her father's study where she slept on a pull-out couch and got her backpack, emptying out the books and pencils and dirty gym clothes on the floor. In the pocket of her backpack, she stuffed four pairs of panties, two pairs of panty hose with diamond glittery stuff running up the legs, and the big-breasted bra.

The next article of clothing she pulled out of the bag was a navy-blue dress. It was almost her size, so it must have belonged to someone quite tiny. The dress was strapless, with embroidered daisies along the bottom of the short-short skirt, and made from a slinky material, slightly elastic.

Blister stripped off her clothes and looked at herself naked in the long mirror on her father's closet door.

She was skinny, so skinny her hipbones stuck out like triangles. Her long curly hair was particularly red with the sun shining through the window — the color of pomegranates — and her small face was peppered with freckles. Her father told her she was "cute," or sometimes "adorable," a word she preferred. But at school, she wasn't one of the pretty ones, not a girl the boys particularly liked, or one that the girls chose to be a part of their exclusive groups.

Like Daisy G., Blister's mark on the world was a result of energy. She had more pure energy than most ordinary fifth-graders at Bixley Elementary, or anyplace else.

"I wasn't a winner," Daisy G. would tell her, brushing her dyed red hair on top of her head like a Brillo pad, putting Revlon's Apple Surprise lipstick on her prune-dried lips. "But I was always a player. And you're just like me, Alyssa Reed. Never give up, until you're dead as a doornail."

Blister picked up the navy-blue dress and pulled it over her head, so it fell just above the ankles. Her breasts were tiny little knobs, but the Lycra in the strapless dress made the dress tight enough to keep from falling off. She didn't look bad, she decided. She scrambled through the canvas bag and found a zippered bag with makeup, two tubes of lipstick, blush, mascara, and a cover-up stick. The woman who had left her suitcase under Jack Reed's bed probably had pimples, an adolescent acne condition which was why she needed the cover-up.

Blister chose Wine Currant lipstick, not the best shade for a redhead; but all the colors in the makeup bag were purply. She put on some rust-colored blush — a shade darker than her freckles — and stood before the mirror, holding her hair back, lowering her eyes, pushing out her lips in an expression she had seen on the girls in teen magazines at the drugstore. She liked the look. With a sweater, she could imagine herself arriving at Bixley Elementary on Monday morning in her navy-blue strapless.

She checked the bag for shoes and found a perfect pair of shiny leather strappy shoes, high heeled. She put them on.

Whoever had left her suitcase under Jack Reed's bed was not coming back. Not while Blister was there. She could count on that. And suddenly brave, she turned the canvas bag upside down and dumped the contents on the floor.

There were little cotton shorts, and long slinky skirts, and cotton T-shirts, and see-through gauzy tops, and four pairs of high-high heels — hardly ever worn — and a box of jewelry. Blister opened it out on her father's bed, and out spilled gold chains, and bulky earrings, and dozens of skinny wire bracelets in pastel colors, and a gold ring, which Blister put on her index finger.

It was a small gold band, with a sunken red stone in the middle — a ruby, she guessed. She decided to keep it.

She put the rest of the jewelry back in the box and started through the clothes. The shorts were too big; besides, they looked foolish, hanging down on her hips the way they did. On a grown-up, they must have been short enough to show half a woman's bottom. She reached into the pocket of the purple-striped shorts — summer shorts, and here it was October, cold enough for a coat. There was a dime in one pocket, and a plastic barrette with a little strand of hair stuck to it, reddish brown and curly. In the other pocket was a yellow sticky note. "Tamara," it read. "Call me at work as soon as you get this. J."

Blister looked at the note for a long time. The writing

was her father's scrawly script, the kinds of letters that all look the same, half lying down on the page. Tamara. Tamara was the woman, the half-grown girl who wore the little purple-striped shorts, the slinky skirts, the pale-pink gauzy tops. Blister tore the note into tiny confetti pieces, and dropped it on the bottom of the empty canvas bag.

She decided on the navy-blue dress with daisies; a long, hot-pink, slinky skirt with a scalloped hem; a tiny black T-shirt, with TROUBLE written on the front in purple block letters; a thin, silky top in aquamarine, which looked very nice with her red hair; another dress — less formal than the strapless one — a green-and-yellow-flowered print, with buttons all the way down the front; and a yellow cardigan in the softest material she had ever touched.

She took a second pair of high-high heels, wondering as she stuffed them in her backpack, whether anyone in the fifth grade ever wore high heels to school, and if she should wear a pair of the pantyhose with diamonds that she also had put in her backpack. She wondered whether, dressed like this, wearing the strapless, navy-blue slinky as well, she'd be sent home from school with a note for her mother. Or maybe the police would be called. She hoped that would happen.

"Whose clothes are these?" her mother would ask her, when she received the note.

"Tamara's," she would say nonchalantly. "I found them in a suitcase under my father's bed in his new apartment."

Or if the police had been called, and asked her wherever did she get such clothes, and why was she wearing them to school, she would open her eyes wide, and reply with a shrug: "From my father, Jack Reed." And she'd give the police officer her father's address.

Blister zipped up her backpack and slid it in a corner of the living room behind the couch. She dumped the rest of the clothes, not bothering to fold them, back in the canvas bag. Then, thinking that it seemed too empty, she stuffed a pillow from the couch on top, so her father would have no reason to think that someone had been searching through Tamara's things.

Then she organized her books on the dining-room table as if she had spent her father's absence studying. She put on her black trousers, a yellow cotton turtleneck, and high-tops. Finally, she sat down at the dining-room table with *Charlotte's Web* opened to page 4, and waited for her father to return with breakfast.

CHAPTER SIX

Jack Reed burst through the apartment door — one arm full of groceries, the other with unfolded laundry, which he dropped on the couch.

"Breakfast!" he announced taking two hot, buttered bagels wrapped in aluminum out of the bag, a carton of orange juice, and the newspaper, which he put down next to Blister.

Blister looked up from her book. The small gold ring belonging to Tamara was on her index finger, peering between the fingers of her clasped hand.

"It took you forever," she said. "I was beginning to get worried."

"Did it?" Her father opened the newspaper and turned to the sports page. "There was a long line at the bagel place."

She lifted her left hand to her face, placing it just so, in such a position her father couldn't possibly miss the ring.

"I couldn't remember whether you liked honey-wheat bagels or cinnamon-raisin, so I got the cinnamon-raisin because they're sweeter."

"I don't like cinnamon-raisin," she said. "Or honey-wheat either. I only like plain and granola."

Perhaps she should tell him, since he didn't seem to notice.

"So," she could say. "I suppose this ring I found is one you gave to Mama when you were married."

Perhaps he'd notice then. Maybe he'd be angry — even lose his temper — tell her to take it off, to put it back where she had found it.

"Were you studying?" he asked, without mentioning his choice of bagels or the ring.

"I don't need to study at this new school," she said.

"Tell me, how's the social life at school?" he asked,

getting up from his chair. He opened the orange juice carton and poured out two glasses. "You haven't said anything lately."

"The social life's great," Blister said.

"Any new friends?"

"Tons," she said, putting her hand with the ring in her lap, giving up on the idea that her father might notice it.

"That's terrific news." He unwrapped the silver paper from the bagels and put them on a plate. "I knew you'd make new friends in a hurry."

She rested her chin in her hands.

"I get asked over to someone's house almost every night of the weekend," she said casually.

"Swell. I'm not at all surprised."

It wasn't true, of course. So far — and it was already October — she hadn't been asked over to anybody's house once, not even to Rylynda Revere's birthday party, to which every girl in the class was invited as far as Blister could tell.

At first, the fifth-graders at Bixley Elementary had been fascinated by her. They liked her name, her "everything's fine" attitude, the "don't worry about me" kind of swing to her walk. They wanted to know all about Lila Rose and the horses and dogs and whether her sister had died all of a sudden.

"All of a sudden," Blister said, assuming a role of invented self-confidence at which she was excellent.

But gradually the fifth-grade girls fell back into their old friendships, slipped into private circles to tell their old secrets back and forth, paying little attention to Blister, who didn't appear to need their attention at all. They weren't exactly mean, but they clustered together in small groups, as they had on the first day of school — glued to one another, whispering and giggling. No room for Blister to slip between them, to find a way into the circle. Just like Sara Barton had promised. She had been dropped like a hot potato, as Daisy G. would say.

"Where have you been invited?" her father asked.

"Like last weekend I was at Shelly Cooke's, and two girls asked me for tonight — but I couldn't go, because I was coming here."

"But I don't want to keep you from your friends, sweetheart," her father said.

"I can see my friends every day at school," she said. "I only see you occasionally."

Her father turned the newspaper over, then pushed back his chair and crossed his legs, his arms folded across his chest in an attitude for listening.

"So tell me about these new friends," he asked.

Blister shrugged, spreading cream cheese on her bagel. "There's Veronique — I don't know her last name — and Molly True, and Sally Teabrook, and Mary Sue Otter, and Bylynda Revere, and Anne Ballou — and I mean, there are so many, I can't even count."

"That's wonderful, sweetheart," her father said, checking his watch. He put on his sweatshirt. "We better get ready to go, or all the bikes will be rented by the time we get to the park. It's after nine-thirty."

The bike-rental shack was just off the highway at the beginning of the bike path, which meandered along the river and through the woods to a large playground. There were food kiosks where you could get ice cream and Slurpees and soft drinks and pretzels, and tables where families out for a Saturday together ate lunch in fine weather.

"We'll ride to the park and eat," her father had said. "Then the movies."

When they got to the bike-rental place, the smaller bikes were gone, so they had to wait while a boy — quite a good-looking boy, with a broad dimple in one cheek and wild blond curls — adjusted a bike for Blister. Then they waited while her father tried out bikes, testing to see whether he liked the feel of them.

"We're only going to ride for a little while," Blister said. She was worried that one of the girls in her class might ride by with her parents, and then Blister would have to introduce the girl to her father and her father would know, by the way the girl behaved, that she and Blister were not truly friends.

"I like a perfect fit," her father had said, trying a second bike, a red Schwinn.

The blond boy rolled his eyes.

"He's like that," Blister said, as he rode around the shed. "I can't help it."

"Not this one," her father said, returning the bike to the boy. "Too unsteady. You shouldn't be renting bikes like this. You could have a lawsuit."

The gear shift of the third bike he tried was too difficult to change, and the next one had a flat tire by the time he had taken a practice run around the parking lot.

"Please," Blister said, when he returned the bike with a flat tire. "We'll never get to the movies."

So he finally agreed to rent a mountain bike with squeaky brakes and Blister followed him along the river, keeping just behind.

It was cold and damp by the river, a light wind

depositing drops of dew on Blister's cheeks. Almost from the beginning she wanted the bike ride to be over.

She wanted the day, even the weekend, with her father to be over, so she could go home to her own bedroom and try on Tamara's clothes.

She was riding toward the park with her head down, focused on the back of her father's bike and imagining herself in the slinky pink skirt and strappy high heels, with her hair in a high ponytail when, out of the corner of her eye, she saw Anne Ballou and Veronique riding toward her from the other direction.

"Blister!" Anne called, in a high-pitched voice, screeching to a stop.

Blister slowed down.

"Hi," Blister said, thinking quickly of what to possibly say so her father would think they were the good friends she had just mentioned to him. "I meant to call you last night about cheerleading."

"Cheerleading?" Anne asked.

"I think tryouts start on Monday."

"They do," Veronique said.

"Are you trying out?" Anne asked. "I didn't think you were."

"I am trying out," Blister said. "I've been practicing."

"Practicing where?" Veronique asked.

"Just by myself at home. I'm pretty good."

Ahead, her father had stopped and turned his bike around.

"We've been practicing all summer, in Bylynda's back-yard on Fesseden Street," Veronique said. "A bunch of us every afternoon, unless it's raining."

"Oh, right," Blister said breezily. "Bylynda asked me if I wanted to practice too, but I've been so busy with other junk that I haven't been able to make it."

There wasn't any truth to what she said. Bylynda had never once called Blister since she'd arrived at Bixley Elementary. They had hardly spoken, except for the con-versation on the playground the first day of school. Maybe Anne would tell Bylynda she'd seen Blister on the bike path, and Bylynda would say, "I've never called Blister Reed in my life."

But so what? Blister thought to herself. At least her fa-ther *thought* she had been invited to someone's house, and that was worth lying for, she decided, as she rode off in the other direction away from the Bixley group.

She ordered a Slurpee and hot pretzel for lunch and

her father ordered a garden salad and two apples. And while they were waiting for the food to come, her father did thirty sit-ups and thirty push-ups, then sat on the ground doing leg stretches.

It drove Blister crazy. He acted as if he were planning to try out for the high-school track team.

"You didn't used to be an athlete," she said.

"I'm not an athlete now," he replied, out of breath. "I'm just getting in shape."

"So tell me about cheerleading," her father asked later, after the movies and popcorn for dinner, as they pulled into the parking lot of his apartment. "Is it a big deal?"

"The biggest," Blister said.

"And you want to be a cheerleader?"

"What else?" Blister asked, getting out of the car and following her father into the building. "I *have* to be one."

"How are your chances?" He turned the key in the lock to the apartment.

"Pretty good," Blister shrugged. "I'm probably the third- or fourth-best."

Which was true. She was quick, and agile, and good at jumps and leaps and cartwheels. She was especially good at enthusiasm.

"So, just like your mother who was a cheerleader, you'll probably be chosen."

"I hope," she said, matter-of-factly.

When Jack Reed finally noticed the gold ring on Blister's finger, they were sitting on the couch watching the late-night news.

"Did I give this to you?" he asked, taking her hand and looking at the ruby ring under the light, as if he actually didn't remember.

What was he thinking? Blister asked herself. Surely he knew whose ring it was. He must have seen it a million times on Tamara's hand. He might even have bought it for her. But then, of course, her father had trouble remembering anything, so perhaps he had forgotten this too.

"Nope," she said, sliding down in the couch, her arms around her knees. "You didn't give it to me."

"Where did you get it?"

"You gave it to Mama," Blister said.

She said it easily — "you gave it to Mama" — giving her answer no thought at all, not even certain where the story had come from. "And later, Mama gave it to me."

"I guess I had forgotten," he said, clicking the remote.

The television went dark. He turned off the light beside the couch and got up.

"Almost midnight. Time for bed," he said. "Your mother will murder me for letting you stay up so late."

"No, she won't," Blister said, which was perfectly true, since her mother slept most of the day and didn't know daylight from darkness any longer.

"Then it's time for me to go to bed," he said.

Blister could feel him watching her as she walked toward the study where she slept. Probably he was beginning to re-member the ring, remembering that he had not given a gold ring with a tiny jewel in the middle to Mary Reed. He hadn't given it to anyone, hadn't even bought it with his own money. Instead he had seen it on the fashion queen, Tamara.

She took off her clothes, put on a large T-shirt which hung to her knees, and climbed into her sleeping bag on the pull-out couch, slipping her hand with the ring under her pillow.

Some nights since the baby died, when Blister couldn't sleep, she imagined a sister. Older, twenty or so, a dancer like Daisy G. — only a real dancer, very tall, with long legs, her hair pulled back tight in a chignon — who came into her bedroom at night and kissed Blister good night, the way her mother used to do before the baby died.

CHAPTER SEVEN

When Blister arrived home on Sunday, after the weekend with her father, her mother was sleeping on the couch. The television was tuned to a Sunday news show, but her mother wasn't watching. Her eyes were closed, her hair scrambled in a yellow nest as if she never combed it, her lips slack, falling away from her teeth. It was afternoon, and she was still in her nightgown.

Blister couldn't bear to look at her — a woman who had been beautiful, with curly blond hair, a sweet and pretty face. Her speckled eyes, once the color of a summer day, were gray now as if a thin film had washed across them, stolen the color from the iris.

"Any calls?" Blister asked.

Her mother opened her eyes, smiling weakly.

"No calls," she said.

"That's funny," Blister said, stricken that her mother didn't even care that she had received no calls, that no one ever called her since she'd moved to Bixley Elementary. She dropped her bookbag full of Tamara's clothes at the door to her room, and headed for the kitchen. "I was expecting Bylynda to call, to tell me where cheerleading practice is today."

"Bylynda?"

"My friend from school. We practice in her backyard on Fesseden Street," she called from the kitchen, opening the door to the fridge which was nearly empty, except for a mealy pear and some jam. She took the pear and cut it up, taking half to her mother.

"Did you have fun at your father's?"

"Boring," Blister said, knowing it was what her mother wanted to hear. "Nothing to do. Nowhere to go, except the bowling alley." She told her mother that her father had been in a bad mood, sulking in front of the television.

"What did you do?"

"Practically nothing." She sat down on the end of the couch. "Watched TV, stuff like that. His apartment's a wreck."

"Messy?"

"Just a junky old apartment, with hardly any furniture. What you'd expect from a man living by himself."

"So you don't think he has a girlfriend?"

The only time her mother showed any of the spirit that Blister remembered from the time before the baby died, was after Blister visited her father. Then her mother wanted to know everything. What she'd eaten, where they'd gone, what her father had said, what the apartment looked like, what he wore, and whether he had any new clothes in his closet. She always asked about a girlfriend.

"No evidence of a girlfriend that I've seen," Blister always said.

This visit had been the first evidence of a girlfriend.

Blister leaned back on the couch, a faraway look in her eyes, uncertain of what to say. Maybe a girlfriend would make her mother jealous — and if she were jealous she might fight to get her father back. And win. Then they'd be a family again, move back to the country, get chickens, repossess the cats and the goat, and try for a new baby girl.

On the other hand, maybe the thought of a girlfriend

would make her mother more depressed, and then she'd never turn off the television or get up from the couch.

"I don't know," she said. "I doubt he has a girlfriend."

"You don't know?" her mother asked.

"I don't think he has a girlfriend."

She finished her pear, put her schoolbooks on the dining-room table, where she usually did her homework, and picked up the telephone to call Bylynda.

"Does your father ever mention me?" her mother asked quietly.

"Sometimes," Blister said, dialing Bylynda's number.

She wished her mother wouldn't ask questions like that. What else was she to say? Sometimes her father spoke of Mary Reed — like yesterday — but not often. Not enough to satisfy her mother.

Bylynda answered on the first ring.

"Hi, it's Blister."

"Hi," Bylynda said.

"I was wondering what time cheerleading practice is going to be today."

All the way home from her father's apartment, she had thought about calling Bylynda, practicing her speech. It would be a cheerful, confident speech as if they were old friends or new good friends. If, for example, she called Bylynda and pretended that she had been invited to practice — pretended, perhaps, that Anne had invited her — what could Bylynda say? "Of course," she'd say, "Come on over."

Unless of course, she was pure meanness. Then she might say something like, "Sorry, Blister, you're not invited, so don't come."

Or, "This is a private practice, and only my best friends are here."

Or she could even lie. "I don't know what you're talking about," she might say.

But Blister decided it was worth the risk. She knew Bylynda's telephone number by heart.

"Who told you about practice?" Bylynda asked.

"Anne," Blister said cheerily. "And I told her I could come today because I really need to practice, since tryouts are this week."

Bylynda hesitated.

"I saw Anne when I was biking with my father yesterday."

"And she invited you?" Bylynda asked.

"She told me it's at your house," Blister said.

There was a long hesitation, so long that Blister was certain Bylynda was going to say "Sorry," in that whiny voice she had. But she didn't.

"Do you know where I live?" Bylynda asked, finally.

"In North Springwood," Blister said, full of excitement. "I've got friends in your neighborhood, so I've been there before."

"1848 Fesseden is my adddress," Bylynda said. "Do you know how to get here?"

"I know exactly where you live, and I'll be there on time," Blister said, adding casually, "But I have to leave early, because I have a birthday party."

She certainly wasn't going to let Bylynda think she didn't get invited to birthday parties. She wanted all the girls in the fifth grade to think that she was invited everywhere, all the time, and just didn't have the time to go.

"Whose birthday?"

"Just a friend," Blister said.

"From school?"

"From my old school," she said. "I have a birthday party almost every week."

"Well," Bylynda said. "We start practice pretty soon. Just come down Fesseden. My house is sort of green, with black shutters."

"I know."

Blister did know exactly where Bylynda lived. In September, when she had overheard some of the girls talking about Bylynda's birthday party — to which every other girl in the class had been invited, except maybe Sara Barton — Blister had looked up her address in the telephone book. That afternoon, she had walked twelve blocks out of her way between Bixley Elementary and her own apartment, just to see 1848 Fesseden, hoping to pass Bylynda on the street, to come upon her by surprise.

"Hi," she'd say brightly, when she saw her. "What's up?"

"Not much," Bylynda would reply. "What are you doing in my neighborhood?"

"Just on my way home." Blister would shrug.

And then Bylynda would suddenly remember that she hadn't asked Blister to her birthday party.

"Oh m'god," she'd say. "I'm having a sleepover this Saturday for my birthday, and I want you to come."

"Maybe I'll come," Blister would reply. "If I don't have other plans."

But as it turned out, she didn't see Bylynda or anyone else that she knew from Bixley, only the pale-green wood house with black shutters, and roses in the front garden: 1848 Fesseden.

Blister hung up the phone and headed to her room.

"You didn't mention to me that you were invited to a birthday party," her mother said.

"I made it up," Blister said.

"Lied?"

"No, it's different from lying," Blister said, picking up her backpack. "I made it up. Daisy G. told me that lying is bad, but making things up is sometimes useful," Blister went on. "And it was useful for me to lie to Bylynda Revere."

"Your grandmother has never told me that, about making things up," her mother said.

"You are her daughter," Blister said. "Some things she doesn't think you should know."

"I'm careful with your mama," Daisy G. had told her. "She's fine glass, delicate around the edges. Not like you and me, Alyssa," she'd said. "Pop-up dolls is what we are."

"Sometimes I don't want to be a pop-up doll," Blister had replied.

She picked up her backpack and went into her room, shutting the door behind her.

"I don't like the way you close the door to your bedroom lately," her mother called.

She pretended not to hear, unzipping the backpack, deciding not to dump it on the bed, in case her mother got up from the couch and came into her room.

"You used to tell me everything," her mother said. "Blister?"

"I still tell you everything," Blister replied, pulling one of the long slinky skirts out of the backpack, the iridescent pink one, shimmering gold, and a tiny black T-shirt.

"What are you doing in there?" her mother called.

"Exactly nothing but dressing for cheerleading practice, Mama," Blister said.

She got the makeup bag out, and then she pushed the backpack under her bed.

Her mother had gotten up. She could hear her shuffling across the floor, hesitating at the door to her bedroom and then knocking.

"Come in," Blister said.

Her mother opened the door.

Blister was standing in middle of her room in the pink skirt and black T-shirt and her tennis shoes. She could see herself in the mirror on the back of her closet door and was pleased. Not exactly MTV, but she was sassy, she decided. Nobody could possibly ignore a girl in the fifth grade dressed like this.

"I got them yesterday with Dad," Blister said, before her mother could ask.

"Whatever for?"

"I wanted them. Girls in fifth grade are beginning to dress like this."

"For school?"

"Sometimes for school, and always for cheerleading practice," Blister said. "Some girls go out with boys, you know. The more advanced ones."

Her mother leaned against the door.

"And how 'advanced' would you describe yourself?" she asked.

"In the middle. Straight in the center, on the way to getting advanced," Blister said, thinking how she would get the makeup she'd stuck under her pillow, the high heels, and a sweater, and get out of the house without being caught.

"There're a little big," her mother said. But she was actually smiling, or almost smiling. Her lip was curling. There was a tiny dimple in her cheek.

"You sort of like this look, don't you?" Blister asked.

"I don't mind it," her mother said. "It reminds me a little of myself when I was your age, feeling grown-up."

*   *   *

Blister had been practicing cheerleading in front of the long mirror on her closet door for weeks.

"*Aka-laka-ching. Aka-laka-chow. Aka-laka-ching-ching, chow-chow-chow! Boomeranga, boomeranga, sis-boom-bah! Bixley, Bixley, rah-rah-rah!*"

She'd fling herself across the bedroom, practicing her leaps. She could do cartwheels on one hand, walking handstands, backbends, running somersaults, and baton twirling. Now, standing in her bedroom, examining herself in the long mirror on the closet door, she hoped she had practiced enough — that she wouldn't be embarrassed in front of the other girls.

"I'll be back by dinner," she said to her mother, as she left the apartment. But Mary Reed was lost in her own thoughts, giving Blister a vacant, distant smile, and a slight wave of her hand.

Walking the long mile to Fesseden Street in her shimmering skirt and makeup — blush, Very Black mascara, toffee lip gloss — with the strappy high heels in her backpack, Blister was hopeful that Tamara's clothes would be enough protection against her uncertainty.

CHAPTER EIGHT

When Blister arrived teetering into the backyard in her high-heeled sandals, five girls were sitting on the steps of the back porch of Bylynda's house. Anne was there blowing small, noisy bubbles with her lavender bubble gum. And Bylynda was dressed in an old cheerleading skirt and sweater belonging to her aunt in Texas.

"That's why the maroon 'W,'" Bylynda said, indicating the letter on her sweater. "'W' for Wallou Junior High, in Wallou, Texas."

Mary Sue, her hand cupped over her mouth, was whispering to Veronique. And there was Jess, little round Jess with her sourpuss smile, who had never once been nice to Blister. Never even bothered to speak.

"Where did you get those amazing clothes?" Anne asked, tossing the bubble gum behind the hydrangea bushes.

"Hand-me-downs," Blister said casually, sinking down on the step beside Bylynda.

"Who gave them to you?" Veronique asked. "They're wild."

"My sister," Blister said. "She's a dancer." She paused carefully. "A professional dancer."

"And your mom doesn't go crazy when you dress like that?" Mary Sue asked.

Blister shrugged.

"I have someplace to go after practice," she said. "I need to be dressed up."

"A birthday party," Bylynda explained. "With boys."

"For someone you don't know," Blister said, crossing her skinny legs, hanging one strappy sandal off her foot, the way she'd seen done in the movies.

"My parents are really strict, especially about what I wear. My mom still lays out my clothes every day," Anne said.

"I have a lot of freedom. Pretty much anything I want to do, my mom lets me." Blister leaned back against the porch steps, her eyes half closed, practicing silence.

"If you want to be powerful," Daisy G. had told her, "don't talk."

"How come?" Blister had asked her.

"Think about it, plumcake. Try it out," Daisy G. said. "Silence is not a talent of mine — but I have noticed that the people who lower their eyes and shut their mouths tend to get what they want."

Bylynda moved closer to Blister, assessing her with something like admiration.

"How come you have so much freedom?" Veronique asked.

Blister leaned over to hook the shoe strap on the back of her ankle, her heart beating with excitement and fear.

"Maybe her mother and father trust her," Bylynda said.

"Mine don't," Veronique said. "They even worry when I cross the street."

"This year I'm supposed to be allowed to go to town alone and to the movies," Mary Sue said. "But so far, nothing has changed."

"You really can do anything you want?" Jess asked.

"Sort of," Blister said, softly.

"Without asking?"

Blister raised her eyebrows, folded her arms over her knees.

"Well, I think you're very lucky," Bylynda was saying. "I have zero freedom, unless my mother goes on a trip."

"Me too," Veronique agreed.

"I completely love your clothes," Bylynda said.

"I especially like the shoes." Anne took the one hanging off Blister's foot and tried it on.

"Cool." She stood up and tried walking with one high heel across the lawn.

"So, are we practicing or not?" Veronique did a cartwheel off the steps.

"Practicing," Anne said, dropping the shoe back beside Blister, putting her oxfords back on.

Blister took off her sweater, pulled her long skirt up to a short skirt so it would be easier to do leaps, and changed her shoes to the Nikes she had packed in her backpack.

Jess was leaning against the wooden steps, watching from under the bill of a blue-and-white baseball cap set square on her head with BIXLEY in red across the front.

"I didn't know you had a sister," she said.

"I do," Blister said.

"I thought you were an only child and your baby sister died," Jess said.

"Well, you're almost right. My sister is a dancer who lives a long way from here, in Cincinnati." Cincinnati was a pretty word. Blister was pleased she'd chosen a name with such authority.

She followed Bylynda into the center of the backyard, lining up to practice.

"Aren't you practicing, Jess?" Bylynda asked, taking her place in the middle, as if she had already been chosen captain.

"I'm going to watch for a while," Jess said.

"Jess is the best," Bylynda told Blister, spreading her arms, instructing the others to follow her. "She doesn't even need to practice."

Blister spread her arms, her fingers touching Anne's fingers.

"Okay?" Bylynda called out.

"Okay," everyone replied.

"Ready? One. Two. Three!" Bylynda faced them, her arms folded across her chest, her head high. "*Aka-laka-ching. Aha-laha chow Aka laka ching-ching, chow-chow-chow! Boomeranga, boomeranga, sis-boom-bah! Bixley, Bixley, rah-rah-rah!*"

Blister followed easily — jumping higher than anyone, her arms perfect, her legs arched in a U behind her — feeling wonderful, almost, for a moment, like her old self before she moved to Bixley, at ease, happy, a part of the group.

Bylynda cocked her head.

"That's okay. Except Anne, you're a little too slow, and Blister, you're a little too fast."

"But you're really good, Blister," Anne said.

"Almost like the cheerleaders at the football games on television," Mary Sue said.

"Thank you," Blister said, her face flushed.

"Now, cartwheels," Bylynda said. "After we finish Aka-Laka-Ching, we do cartwheels," Bylynda said, speaking specifically to Blister. "Can you do a cartwheel?"

"I'm okay with cartwheels," Blister said.

"One-handed?"

"I think," Blister said. She could do one-handed very easily. She had practiced a million times in her tiny bedroom in the new apartment while her mother was half-sleeping in front of the TV. She could almost do a no-handed cartwheel.

"I'll try," she said, taking off, sailing around the edges of Bylynda's garden so quickly it was hard to see whether she was upside down or right side up. Then one-handed — left first, then right — and two flips without hands — one, two, and up, stretching her arms in the air.

"Bixley, Bixley, go, go, go!" she shouted.

Bylynda shrugged.

"Not bad."

"You're really good," Veronique said.

"Thank you," Blister said, bowing, so full of pleasure that she walked on her hands across the yard, over to the steps where Jess was standing.

"I'm amazed," Veronique said. "And we've all been practicing since July."

"Can you walk up the steps on your hands?" Jess asked, coolly.

"Probably," Blister said, out of breath.

She had never tried walking up the steps on her hands, *But why not?* she thought. Her arms were strong enough. One arm at a time balancing the full weight of her body. Of course she could do it.

"I'll try it." She felt Jess's eyes on her.

"Then do it," Jess said.

Blister lifted her right hand, putting it on the first step, then shifted her weight slightly forward to the right arm, pushing off with the left hand to bring it up to the first step alongside the right. She almost lost her balance and toppled to the right, but caught herself, her legs waving side to side, her arms steady on the first step.

Behind her, they were clapping.

"How many steps?" she asked.

"Five," Jess said.

But even before Blister lifted her right arm, she knew that she was going to fall. Her balance was off, her arm not quite strong enough to hold her weight. In the process of going up to the second step, her right arm turned to Jell-O, and she fell over backward.

She hurt her back, twisted her arm, slapped her cheek against the bottom step.

"I had a cramp in my arm," she said, standing quickly, turning to face the other girls, her back to Jess. They were watching her, their mouths open in an O of surprise.

"Can anyone else do that?" Bylynda asked, looking down the line of her friends.

"I can do it," Jess said. "Totally easy."

And she flipped upside down, walking up the steps on

her hands as quickly as she might have done walking on her feet.

Blister was the first one to leave after practice. She had a sense that the other girls wanted her to go, that they had plans together and were waiting for her to pack up her things. Not that they were unfriendly, but they weren't particularly friendly either.

"I'm sure you'll make the squad," Anne said, as Blister was changing her shoes.

"Me too," Bylynda agreed.

"No one can do cartwheels as good as you, except Jess — and cartwheels are very important."

"Good luck tomorrow," Anne called, as Blister headed toward the back gate.

"You guys too," Blister said.

"No question you'll make the squad," Veronique said.

"Maybe," Blister said.

And "maybe" is what she felt. Walking the twelve blocks home after practice was over, she tried to imagine herself on the squad, dressed in her short-short cheerleading skirt and white sweater with a maroon "B" for Bixley on the front.

She imagined the gym where tryouts were scheduled to begin on Monday. The gymnasium was full of all the sixth- and fifth-grade girls. She saw herself walk to the middle, stand in front of the crowd, her back straight as a dancer's, her head high, her hair in a ponytail.

"*Aka-laka-ching, Aka-laka-chow, Aka-laka-ching-ching, chow-chow-chow!*"

And she'd do cartwheels like lightning all around the gym, so fast no one could see her legs spinning or her arms twirling — only the splash of color from her skirt, the red of her hair. She'd finish her cartwheels and, for a finale, she'd walk on her hands from the edge of the gym to the center.

She imagined the moment on Tuesday when the names of the new cheerleading squad would be read out in assembly.

"Blister," the principal would say, reading from the list of new cheerleaders, speaking into the microphone. "Blister Reed!"

"Just Blister," she'd say, walking up to the stage in the gym, her face burning red, her heart singing, the crowd cheering so loud she couldn't hear herself think.

But as she rounded the last block, before her own yellow-brick apartment complex loomed ahead, her spirits suddenly fell. In the back of her mind, she heard the voice of Sara Barton at the drugstore, warning her about the popular girls. No matter how good her cartwheels, how high her leaps — there was always a chance, she thought, her excitement draining, that she wouldn't make the squad.

When Blister opened the front door of the apartment in her shimmering skirt and strappy heels, her mother was actually at the door waiting for her.

"Your father called," Mary Reed said, as Blister dropped her backpack on the couch and headed for the kitchen.

"How come?" Blister asked, stopping in the middle of the living room.

"Something has come up," her mother said, and for the first time in forever, since Blister could remember, she seemed almost happy. "He wants you to call him immediately."

CHAPTER NINE

Blister lay on her bed, still in Tamara's clothes, staring into the darkness. In her mind, she was calling her father.

"Hello, Dad. What's up?" she was saying. "Clothes? No, I don't remember any clothes. I mean we were there together at your place the whole time. Where would I have gotten any clothes?"

Outside her closed door, she could hear her mother wandering the apartment, a certain lightness to her step, bustling back and forth as if she had a mission.

"Hello, Dad," Blister was saying in her mind. "Yes. I did see Tamara's suitcase and opened it up, but how was I to know it was Tamara's? And yes, I did take the clothes. I only took the ones I particularly liked, thinking they probably had been bought for me by you as a present, and you just hadn't gotten around to giving them to me yet."

"Hello, Jack. It's Blister," she tried again. "You're wondering if I stole Tamara's clothes. You bet I did. I took everything I wanted, and left the rest of the junk for Tamara. Certainly not. I have no intention of giving them back. Already I've given the gold ring with the little red ruby to Mama, and I gave the makeup away to a homeless woman who lives by the drugstore. She needed some makeup to perk up her day."

"Blister?" Her mother had stopped outside her door.

"Yes, Mama."

"Did you call your father?"

"Not yet."

"He needs to talk to you tonight."

"I'll call him, Mama. But first I'm resting."

"Can I come in?"

"No," Blister said. "In a minute."

There was, of course, the possibility that her father was calling to tell her that he and Tamara were finished.

"Thanks a lot for taking those clothes," he would say. "And especially the gold ring. Tamara and I are kaput."

Blister imagined Tamara arriving at her father's apartment on Sunday afternoon, looking for the suitcase she'd left under the bed.

"Oh my god, Jack!" Tamara would say, dumping her suitcase upside down on the couch. "Somebody's been through my clothes."

"Nobody's been here," her father would have said. "Just me. And what in the world would I want with your clothes?"

"Alyssa spent the weekend."

"Alyssa would never take anything. I know my daughter very well and she would never steal."

"She's stolen from me!" Tamara would say, falling in a heap on the couch in tears. "My beloved strapless dress, my darling little pink skirt, my favorite T-shirt with TROUBLE written on the front, my aquamarine silk top, my makeup bag."

"I'm sure you're wrong, Tamara," Jack Reed would have said. "You don't know Alyssa worth beans."

"You're exactly right. I don't know Alyssa at all," Tamara would wail. "And I hope I never do!"

"What did you say, Tamara?"

"You heard me," Tamara said.

"I certainly did," Jack Reed said. "And no one, not even you, can say anything against my darling daughter. Now, pack your bags and leave immediately."

Turning on the light beside her bed, Blister was feeling cheerful. She imagined the terrible, miserable, teeny little Tamara, packing her canvas bag with what was left of her clothes, and walking out the door of her father's apartment forever. The daydream pleased her.

When the telephone call from her father came, Blister was taking off Tamara's clothes and hanging them in her closet to wear to school the next day.

Her mother knocked.

"For you," she said.

"Dad?"

"Yes."

Blister put on a long T-shirt and settled on the living-room couch, her heart beating, her brain a little scrambled. She was not at all sure what she would say. She picked up the phone.

"Hello?"

"Alyssa?"

"Yes?"

She decided to speak in a refrigerator voice, as if her father were a stranger interrupting her evening at home.

"There's a problem."

"What problem?"

She was thinking that if this conversation could go on very, very slowly, perhaps nothing important would happen. He might even forget why he had called.

"You know what problem I'm talking about."

"I don't think I *do* know," Blister said.

"Then I'll remind you."

"Okay." She folded her legs under her and held the telephone a distance from her ear so her father's voice was muted.

"There was a suitcase under my bed, and you opened it and took some things out," Jack Reed was saying. "Apparently you have taken the things home."

"A suitcase?"

She could hear her father's exasperation.

"Could you describe what's missing?" she asked.

"I couldn't describe what's missing. But it's missing. That's all I know."

"Are the clothes yours?" Blister asked casually.

"Of course they're not my clothes. They're not men's clothes."

She could tell that her father was pacing his apartment, running his hand through his black hair as he had a tendency to do when he was nervous or angry.

"Then who could they belong to?"

Her father's voice dropped to the bottom of a well.

"I'll pick them up tonight," he said. "I'll be over shortly."

"Well, you probably won't see me because I'm going to bed. I need to get up early for cheerleading."

"Then give them to your mother."

And he hung up.

"What was that about?" her mother asked.

"Dad's coming over to pick something up."

"He is?"

"That's what he said. But I'm exhausted, so I'm going to bed."

In her bedroom, she went through some of the clothes she had taken from Tamara. Stolen clothes. She had taken them without a single thought, without a moment of guilt or sympathy for Tamara, or even worry about herself as a newborn criminal. As far as Blister was concerned, Tamara, in her tiny little dresses and shiny skirts, had stolen her father — so it was Blister's right, maybe even her obligation, to take Tamara's clothes away from her father's apartment. She certainly wasn't going to give *all* of them back, just because she'd been caught. She needed something to wear for tomorrow that would make everyone notice her — something sassy and grown-up, the way she felt in Tamara's slinky skirt. So she got a paper bag from the kitchen and stuffed most of Tamara's clothes in the bottom. Then she folded the bag, taped it shut, and put it beside the front door. She kept the gold ring, but not the makeup. After all — she should have thought about this earlier — the lipstick had been on Tamara's lips.

Her mother wasn't lying on the couch, as she usually was, when Blister went into the living room, and the door to her bedroom was shut.

"Mama?" Blister called.

"Just a minute, sweetheart."

"Can I come in?"

"Not just now. I'll be out in a second."

Blister leaned against the wall, listening to the sounds of dressing behind the door.

"Are you okay, Mama?" she asked.

"I'm fine," her mother said.

"Really fine?"

"Really fine," her mother said, and she sounded almost cheerful.

Fine. It was the first time in months — since the baby, since Jack Reed had moved into his own apartment, that Blister had heard her mother's voice full of life again.

She folded her arms across her chest and waited.

It was quite a long wait and she began to worry that her father would arrive to pick up Tamara's clothes and there she'd be, standing outside her mother's bedroom. And then she'd have to talk to him. She'd have to explain that she'd taken the clothes because they were under his bed and, because he was *her* father, she somehow had a right to them. Or maybe she should have given the clothes away to her mother, who was after all his wife.

And that was the way Blister's mind was traveling when the door to her mother's room opened and there she was, looking so beautiful, it took Blister's breath away.

"Mama!"

Her mother had on a long, gray skinny skirt and a bright red turtleneck and makeup. She had not worn makeup in months. Her cheeks were glowing, her hair full and shiny. She was actually smiling.

"You look perfect."

"Thank you, Alyssa."

"Are you dressed up because Dad is coming over?"

"I didn't want to look like a witch."

"He'll be so happy to see you."

"I hope so."

"He will. I completely know that."

When her father arrived, Blister was in her bedroom with the door locked, just in case he opened the paper bag to check the merchandise and wanted to speak to her. She lay on the floor next to the door, listening under the crack at the bottom. She could hear them talking, her father particularly, although she couldn't make out her mother's words, only the lilting sound of her voice.

"Alyssa simply opened a suitcase and stole things that didn't belong to her," her father was saying.

Her mother said something in response that Blister couldn't hear, and her father must have interrupted in the middle of her sentence.

"It doesn't matter whose clothes they are, Mary. What matters is that your daughter has broken the law."

"*Our* daughter."

Blister could hear that clearly.

"I want to speak to her."

Blister heard her father walk across the room, saw his shoes under the crack. He was wearing tennis shoes and dirty white socks. He tried the door.

"Alyssa?"

"She's sleeping," her mother said.

"She's not sleeping, Mary. She couldn't be sleeping. She's peering under the door, listening."

Blister heard a flutter of activity, the crackling of paper, no one talking and then her father saying in a terrible voice: "Knock on the door, Mary, and make her give me the gold ring that she stole."

"What ring?" her mother asked, softly.

"She took a gold ring with a ruby, and I can't find it in these things she's packed."

Her mother didn't reply.

"Alyssa?" He banged on the door.

Blister was standing on the other side of the door.

"Open the door now, and give me the gold ring you lied about."

She moved to the other side of the room, got down on the floor, and crawled under her bed.

"Alyssa?" He banged again, shouting her name: "Alyssa Reed!"

The telephone rang, and there was silence. Blister heard the front door open and close. Then nothing — not even the sound of her mother pacing.

She crawled out from under the bed, tiptoed across the room, and listened against the door to the silence. Then she slipped out and went into the living room, which was dark. Her mother was standing at the window by the dining-room table, looking out into the darkness, her back to Blister.

"Mama?"

Mary Reed didn't answer.

"What happened?"

"A neighbor called me to say there was too much noise coming from our apartment, and so your father left."

"I'm sorry you had to hear all that about the clothes."

"Never mind," her mother said, turning around. She had been crying. "Did you steal them?"

"No, I didn't really steal them," Blister said. "Those clothes shouldn't have been under my father's bed."

"But they weren't yours."

"I was trying to fix things."

Her mother went into the kitchen and poured a glass of water.

"I know you were, Alyssa," she said, going into her room. "And that was very sweet of you. But some things can't be fixed."

CHAPTER TEN

Blister wore the TROUBLE T-shirt and the slinky skirt to school under her jacket. She put the strappy heels in her backpack, planning to change in the girls' room before homeroom. She wished she'd kept some lipstick. She imagined herself arriving in the class dressed up, blush, lipstick, her strappy heels, her fine clothes. That would be a great surprise for the fifth-graders at Bixley Elementary. They'd be amazed.

"Did *you* see Blister?" Anne would say.

"Incredible," Veronique would say. "I've never seen a fifth-grade girl in lipstick at school."

"I'm going to get some pink frosty lip gloss and a slinky skirt and high heels from my mother," Anne would say. "I think we all should."

"Your mother would let you go to school like that?" Bylynda would ask.

"Probably."

"Not my mother," Bylynda would say.

"Blister can do anything she wants to do," Anne would say.

A trendsetter: ahead of her time, sassy, independent. A child model like the girls in the teen magazines she sometimes read at the drugstore.

Of course she'd be selected to be a cheerleader. At least, she had her fingers crossed.

Late the night before, after her mother had gone to bed, Blister had called Daisy G. The clock in the kitchen said midnight but when she answered, music was, as usual, playing in the background and her grandmother was wide-awake.

"Let me just turn this music down," Daisy G. said, clicking across the bare floor. "You hear my tango shoes? I'm practicing for a contest next month."

The music stopped.

"So what's up, treetop?"

"Terrible things are happening at home."

"Oh, what bad luck," Daisy G. said sweetly. "Tell me. Don't spare the truth."

And Blister told her everything, about the clothes and her father, and her mother dressing up for him — and how, after he'd left, her mother had told her that things could never be fixed.

"So what should I do?" Blister asked.

"Go to bed right now and get your beauty sleep. Then in the morning put on your slinky skirt, and go to school for cheerleading tryouts."

"What about my stealing?"

Daisy G. was quiet.

"I know I should feel terrible, but I don't. I don't feel a bit guilty."

"That may be true, pudding, but you shouldn't have taken that Tootsie woman's clothes."

"Tamara."

"I don't like the name Tamara," Daisy G. said. "It spells trouble."

"I was hoping she would pack what was left in her stupid suitcase, and leave my father's apartment forever."

"Of course you were hoping that," Daisy G. said, "but you know we can't control what other people do, sweetheart."

"So you agree with Mama, that things can't be fixed?"

"I don't know about that. They probably can't ever be the way they were before the baby."

"I guess," Blister said.

"But think of it this way, Alyssa. You're only ten, and there's a lot you can do about yourself."

"Like what do you mean?"

"Like a lot of things," Daisy G. said. "A person makes a decision. When your grandfather died, my heart was broken in two. And I said to myself, I can either lie here all day with my shattered heart, or get up and become a famous dancer — husband or not."

"And that worked out?"

"I didn't get famous, as you know," she said. "But I am a dancer."

Mary Reed was in bed when Blister left for school. Blister knocked on the door to her bedroom, opened the door, and looked in. Her mother was turned away from the door, lying on her side.

"I hope cheerleading goes well," her mother called, in her gloomy voice.

"It will," Blister said, imagining her mother on the couch, still in her nightgown, when she came home after school.

Unless, Blister thought, standing in the middle of the living room, she could do something to fix things.

She went back into her bedroom, opened the second drawer of the dresser, and reached into the back of her underwear and sock drawer, where she had slipped the ring with the tiny ruby so her father couldn't find it.

Then she took a piece of lined school paper and wrote:

Dear Mama,
    This is for you.
    Love,
    Alyssa (now Blister)

She put the ring and the note in an envelope, wrote *Mary Reed* on the front, put it on the dining-room table, and left.

Jess was in the girls' room when Blister changed to her strappy heels.

"Is what you're wearing supposed to be a costume?" Jess asked, leaning against the door to the cubicle, watching Blister in the mirror over the sink.

"I'm just sick of jeans and turtlenecks," Blister said. "Everybody in the fifth grade looks exactly the same, like there's only one store in America, and that's where we go shopping."

Jess shrugged. "So, are you trying out for cheerleading today?" she asked.

"Aren't you?"

"I've got a lot of things going on, and I don't know if I'll have the time for cheerleading," Jess said.

"I know what you mean. Like I'm taking dancing."

"What kind?"

"Modern and jazz. That's what these shoes are for." Blister followed Jess out of the girls' room.

"You could get into trouble, dressing like that at school," Jess said.

"Maybe so. No big deal." Blister shrugged. As she was walking, a little wobbly, into the fifth-grade classroom, the principal called down the hall to her.

"See? It's the shoes," Jess said. "You're in trouble."

But it wasn't about the shoes.

"Your father called," Ms. Hartman said.

"How come?"

"He's coming to school to see you about something important. I have agreed that when he comes, you may leave language arts for a while."

Her head felt suddenly woozy.

"And Alyssa?"

"Yes?"

"Did your mother see you leave for school today?"

Blister nodded.

"In those shoes?"

"Not exactly," Blister said.

"I'd like you to change your shoes for school, please."

"I wear them for dancing," Blister said, quietly.

"But you won't be dancing at school."

She put the strappy heels on the shelf in her locker and changed to the Nikes she had packed for tryouts. She tied the laces slowly, taking time before she went into homeroom to think what she was going to do, her stomach wild with butterflies.

Certainly she didn't want to see her father. Not now. Not for a very long while.

In language arts, while everyone else was writing a composition on the meaning of All Hallows' Eve, Blister wrote a letter to her father.

Dear Jack Reed,

I am writing to tell you that I don't like you as much as I used to like you when you were married to my mother, and I don't want to come to your apartment any longer, and I don't like the new friends you've made since you moved away.

If the reason why you're here today at my own school — where I'm very busy with my schoolwork and cheerleading practice — is to talk about stealing, forget it.

I was brought up to believe that if something is broken, you have to fix it.

Yours sincerely,

Blister

She folded the letter in half, raised her hand, and asked to be excused to deliver the letter to the principal's office. At the front desk, she asked the secretary next to the principal's office to give it to her father when he arrived.

Then she went to the girls' room located in the basement across from the kindergarten room, two floors down from the fifth-grade classrooms. She slipped into one of the cubicles and sat on the toilet with the door locked, her feet up, so no one would know she was there.

She figured that she would stay until the bell for recess rang, and then she'd go back to the classroom. That would give her father plenty of time to come to school and read the letter and leave.

She leaned her head against the wall and closed her eyes, practicing cheers for tryouts over and over in her head.

Time passed slow as honey.

Once she thought she heard someone calling her name in the downstairs corridor, and several times a girl came into the bathroom. One pulled on the door to Blister's cubicle.

"The door's locked," the girl told her friend.

"Climb under," the other little girl said.

"I don't have to go anymore," the first one said.

And then they left.

She had almost fallen asleep, leaning against the wall in the cold, damp bathroom, when the bell for recess rang.

"Where have you been?" Ms. Covington asked, when she came back in the classroom. "Your father came to find you."

"I left a note for him. He must have gotten it," Blister said sweetly.

"He needed to see you," she said. "We looked all over. Bylynda went to the girls' room and the gym and the lunchroom."

"I was in the girls' room. I've had a sort of stomach flu today, but it's over now."

"Your father wanted me to tell you that he'll pick you up in front of the school this afternoon at three o'clock."

"Thank you," Blister said, packing her books for science class. She certainly didn't plan to meet Jack Reed in front of Bixley Elementary after classes. In fact, she didn't want to see him again *ever*, until he fixed their lives.

Tryouts did not start off well. It had begun to rain — a thin, gray rain — and the air was chilly, so the gym teacher decided to hold the tryouts in the gym.

When Blister arrived in her Nikes and short-short skirt and sweater, she was already late.

First she couldn't find her language arts homework, and then the principal had stopped her to ask where she had been when her father arrived to meet with her and was everything all right?

"Fine," she'd said. "I left my father a letter."

"We gave him the letter and he read it," Ms. Hartman said. "But he said he needed to see you. We looked all around and couldn't find you."

"You must have missed me," Blister said cheerily,

wondering what her father was thinking now that he'd read her letter. "I was here."

The principal wouldn't let her go, although she was already late for tryouts. She asked all about Blister's life, and the baby, and her parents' separation, and whether things were going well at school, until it was getting late for tryouts.

"Everything is perfectly fine," Blister replied, to every question. Fine, fine, fine.

"Are you sure?" the principal asked.

"Positive," Blister said, slinging her backpack over her shoulder, flashing a bright smile. "Everything in my life is great, almost — except I haven't made the cheerleading squad yet."

And she walked down the corridor toward the gymnasium, thinking it was none of Ms. Hartman's business what was going on in Blister Reed's life, as long as she didn't cause trouble at Bixley Elementary School.

When she finally got to the tryouts, her friends — or her about-to-be-friends, or maybe-friends — were sitting in a pack on the bleachers talking in loud whispers, which she could almost, but not quite, hear. She waved, and they waved back. She went over to the bleachers and sat next to

Bylynda, who said "Hi" in a bored kind of way, already talking to Jess, who was sitting on the bench putting on her Nikes.

A lot of people had come to watch. Ms. Covington was there, sitting at the end of the bench; and Sara Barton, her arms folded tightly across her chest, stood at the edge of the gym; and Ms. Hartman was there with a clipboard, talking to the gym teacher. Some of the parents were standing at the entrance to the gym, far away from their children.

"It's a big deal," Veronique said, sitting next to Blister. "Everybody's here. Even my mom and Aunt Grace."

"I'm surprised that Ms. Hartman is here," Blister said.

"Right, and Ms. Covington too," Veronique agreed. "Is your mom here?"

Blister shook her head. "I didn't tell her to come."

"You probably didn't want her watching you. I didn't want my mom here."

"Me neither."

But Blister would have liked her mother to be there. Not this new mother but the one from last year, who rode her bike all over Meadowville waving to the children in Blister's class, dressed in her blue jeans and baseball cap, and looking hardly older than a child herself.

"So here we go," Mary Sue said, plopping down next to Blister. "I'm so nervous that I threw up after lunch."

"I'm pretty nervous too," Blister said.

"Don't talk about it," Bylynda said, clapping her hands over her ears. "I'm going to faint."

Tryouts were long. One fifth-grade girl after the next — fifteen in all — walked to the center of the gym and did her routine. Blister was fourth from the last.

Already it was clear that Jess would make the squad, and probably Bylynda. But not Veronique — who couldn't do a cartwheel — or Mary Sue, who was so nervous she had to rush out of the gym in the middle of her routine.

"Blister Reed," the gym teacher called out.

Blister walked to the middle of the gym, her back very straight, a spring to her step as if she were absolutely sure of herself, which she was not. But she was very good. Her cartwheels were swift and beautiful, her leaps high in the air, and her arms as straight as a dancer's. Her walk on her hands to the center of the gym brought cheers from the crowd. She was near perfect. Probably even better than Jess.

In the last tryout, a small girl called Melanie fell during her first cartwheel and cried. She left the gym holding Ms.

Covington's hand, while the gym teacher spoke into the microphone, explaining the procedure for voting for the cheerleading squad.

"Now," she said, passing out scraps of paper and pencils. "All the girls and the teachers at Bixley get to vote. You write down the names of five girls in order of preference."

Blister voted. She choose Jess first, Bylynda second, and Mary Sue third — even though Mary Sue was nervous, she was very good. In fourth, she voted for a girl called Barbie, who was the best at leaps. She thought of voting for herself fifth, but it seemed the wrong thing to do. Besides, she was certain she would be chosen. Today at tryouts, she had been better than anyone.

"Did you vote for yourself?" Veronique asked, as they were walking out of the gym.

"No," Blister said. "Did you?"

"Of course. I voted for myself first. Everyone does," Veronique said, and she rushed off to catch up with Jess and Bylynda as they left the gym.

Blister walked home alone. By the time she had packed her books and put on her coat and got out to the front of Bixley Elementary — checking first from the front door to be certain her father's car wasn't waiting outside, everyone seemed to have left, except Sara Barton.

"I'd walk home with you, except I have a dentist appointment," Sara said. "So good luck in getting elected to the squad."

"Thanks," Blister said.

"I think it's probably going to be Jess and Bylynda and Veronique and Mary Sue Otter and Barbie."

"You're probably right." But Blister didn't believe her. In spite of Sara Barton's gloomy predictions, she still believed she would be chosen. Unless everyone who had tried out voted only for herself and the four most popular girls.

CHAPTER ELEVEN

Daisy G. stopped her car on Market Street, three blocks from the apartment, and picked Blister up. It was still gray and raining, the afternoon light fading. Blister was happy to see her grandmother's old blue Toyota at the corner of Market and Sixth. She was soaked to the skin, exhausted from the excitement of tryouts.

"Get in," Daisy G. said, not in a cheerful humor. "On the double."

"How come?" Blister dragged her backpack over the seat and closed the door.

"Trouble," Daisy G. said.

"With what?"

"Your mother isn't in the apartment."

"She was sleeping when I left this morning," Blister said thinly, the breath gone out of her.

"I talked to her after you left for school. She told me you had cheerleading tryouts, and she wasn't feeling well."

"She's never feeling well."

"This time I didn't give her a lecture about pulling up her socks," Daisy G. said. "I didn't even tell her she ought to learn to be more elastic like you and me. Instead I just made chicken soup, and went to the market and got some Hershey's Kisses and a bunch of lavender tulips, and drove over here just after two." She turned the corner into the apartment complex and parked the car. "And when I arrived, your mother wasn't there."

"Did you go in?"

"I knocked and she didn't answer, so I got the super and he opened the front door when I told him it was an emergency. Your mother was gone. The bed was unmade; the dishes were in the sink. I checked her closet, and my guess is she's wearing her gray trousers, and a white turtle-neck, and a windbreaker."

"The blue one," Blister said, her voice measured.

"It's the only one she has."

"Did you call my father?"

"Of course. I called your father and told him I was going to school to pick you up — which I did, but you'd already left — so I drove along the route I thought you'd take walking home, and there you were. I told your father we'd meet back at the apartment."

"Who would meet?"

"You and me and your father."

Blister closed her eyes.

"I can't."

"Of course you can."

"I can't see my father now."

"We're not going to talk about stealing, if that's what you're worried about," Daisy G. said, opening the car door, and taking Blister's hand. "We're going to look for your poor mother. And don't cry."

"I never cry," Blister said.

Daisy G.'s voice softened. "I know you never cry, angel-face. You and me. Tough as nails, even though our hearts are broken in two."

On the way through the parking lot to the apartment building, Blister thought about broken hearts. She had never thought that her heart was broken — and certainly not Daisy G.'s — but she wondered about her mother, worried about her, wished there were something that she could do to make a difference in the way her mother felt every morning when she woke up.

"What about *Mama's* heart?" she asked Daisy G.

"Your mama has been a little bit sad ever since she was young, long before she met your father."

"How come?"

"I'm not sure," Daisy G. said. "I used to think I had so much energy I exhausted your mother. That I took up all the air in the room, and that made her angry. But I don't think that anymore. I just think people are different."

"But you think I'm like you?"

"I say that," Daisy G. said, slipping her hand into Blister's. "I like to think of us together, like a team. But you are really yourself, Alyssa. Just like yourself."

"And that's good?" Blister asked, liking the sound of what her grandmother said.

"That's the best," Daisy G. said.

Blister followed her up the steps of the apartment

building to the second floor. The door was unlocked. Tulips, still wrapped in the florist's paper, were sitting on the dining room table, the apartment empty.

"Your father isn't here yet," Daisy G. said, checking her watch. "Three-thirty. I told him to meet us now."

She took the tulips and put them in a vase, busying about the room, doing the dishes, washing the counters.

"Make your mother's bed, sweetheart. I don't want your father to see this place a mess."

After Blister had made the bed and hung up her mother's nightgown and opened the venetian blinds, letting in the last of the rain-soaked light, she leaned against the door and watched her grandmother work.

"Where do you think she could possibly be?"

Daisy G. shook her head.

"I don't know. I called two of her old friends in Meadowville, and they hadn't spoken to her in weeks. I also called her doctor." She was wiping the dining-room table.

"Maybe she went back to the old house."

"Maybe. We'll go there as soon as your father arrives."

And then, Daisy G. noticed the envelope with *Mary*

Reed written on it, in which Blister had put the gold ring that morning.

"What's this?" she asked.

"What's in it?" Blister said, her heart beating.

Daisy G. turned the envelope upside down and shook it.

"Nothing is in it," she said.

"I put it there this morning, before I left for school," Blister said quietly.

"Was it a note?"

"No," she said. "It was a ring."

"A ring?"

"A ring I'd taken from my father's apartment. I gave it to Mama."

Daisy G. sat down on the couch, folding her arms across her chest. She was so small, her feet barely touched the floor, and were it not for the wrinkles and lines and puffy eyes, a person might mistake her for a child.

"I see."

"When I took those things from the suitcase under my father's bed — you know, the slinky dresses and stuff, there was also this gold ring with a ruby in the center."

"A ruby?"

"I think it's a ruby. It's red."

"And you gave it to your mama."

"I did."

"That was very sweet of you, Alyssa, but —"

"But what?"

"It wasn't yours to give."

Blister shrugged.

"I figured whosever ring it is shouldn't have had their clothes underneath my father's bed."

Daisy G. nodded slowly, her face pensive, her eyes half closed in thought.

"You figured right," she said. "Well, almost right."

When Blister heard her father's steps on the stairs outside the apartment, she rushed into the bathroom and locked the door. She kept the light off, listening, her ear against the door.

Jack Reed was beside himself.

"Beside himself," Daisy G. said to Blister later, after they had looked everywhere in North Haven, even the bowling alley and Jack Reed's new apartment. After they had called all of Mary Reed's friends from Meadowville or left a message on their answering machines. After they had called the police in North Haven, and Blister's old school, and the public library, and the Buy-Rite Market, to see if anyone meeting Mary Reed's description had been there.

Jack Reed even forgot that he was angry at Blister, forgot about Tamara's clothes and the valuable jewelry that Blister had stolen. By the time he had left the apartment to look through North Haven on foot, block by block, he had apologized to Blister and to Daisy G. for moving into his own place and breaking up his family.

It was dark, nearly six o'clock — dinnertime, but no one was hungry, although Daisy G. had just put out the chicken soup — when the telephone rang. The pharmacist from Meadowville was on the phone.

"I got your message to my wife on the answering machine and I may have seen Mary," he said to Daisy G.

Daisy G. knew the pharmacist well. He lived in the house across the street from her apartment. Several times the pharmacist had asked Daisy G. to keep the music down when she played it very loud in the summer. The open windows carried the sound of music into his baby's room.

"I drove up and it looked to me like Mary walking up the steps to your apartment."

"To my apartment?" Daisy G. asked, holding her hand over the receiver and speaking to Blister. "The pharmacist at Bargain Drugs thinks he saw your mama going into my apartment."

"Does she have a key?" Blister asked.

"She always has," Daisy G. said, thanking the pharmacist from the bottom of her heart, and replacing the receiver.

"We'll call her at your house," Blister said, dialing. But the phone rang and rang. No one answered, so Blister finally hung up.

"We're going to Meadowville," Daisy G. said. "Put on your coat, pronto."

The storm had lifted by the time they got to Meadowville, but it was windy and very cold for October. Her mother's car wasn't parked in front of the apartment and, looking up at the second floor where Daisy G. lived, there were no lights. But the apartment was a large one — taking up the whole second floor — so there could have been lights on at the back of the apartment, as Daisy G. said, and the car might be parked in the alley. Daisy G. reached down and took Blister's hand, kissed her fingers.

"Pray," she said.

"I am," Blister said, although she wasn't at all sure how to pray for a lost mother to be found. Or what she should tell God she would give Him in exchange for finding her.

It had been a long, strange day, and Blister was tired to

the bone. Walking up the steps to the apartment, her hand in her grandmother's skinny, bony hand, her legs were almost too heavy to move.

"I'm afraid," she said finally.

"Afraid?" Daisy G. asked. "Of what?"

"Afraid Mama won't be there, and then afraid that maybe she will and something terrible will have happened to her," Blister said, surprised she was able to put into words the thunderstorm of fear that had overtaken her for months like an awful sickness — since the day in Meadowville, after the baby had died, when her mother began to scream and had to be taken away.

"Afraid she's dead?" Daisy G. asked, in her fierce way.

"Something like that," Blister said, so weary she felt as if she might sink to the floor before they got inside the apartment.

"Well, she's not," Daisy G. said. "Count on it. I'm her mother, and I should know."

Daisy G. was right. When she opened the front door of the apartment and went into the foyer and then the large living room overlooking the pharmacist's house, there was a rectangle of light coming from the back of the apartment, falling in a geometric pattern on the floor of the living room, bathing the room in filtered light.

"Mary?" Daisy G. called.

"I'm here, Mama," Mary Reed answered from the bedroom, which was dimly lit.

"We've been looking all over," Daisy G. said.

"I'm sorry," Mary said, coming out of the bedroom then, into the bright lamplight of the living room. She was tentative in her movements, a kind of awkwardness in the way she held herself — less like a woman than a girl.

"Why, Mary Reed. What are you doing in those clothes?" Daisy G. asked quietly, reaching down, taking Blister's hand.

Mary's hair had been cut short in a puff of curls, the way she used to wear it before she got married. She was wearing a very short royal-blue skirt and white cotton socks and a heavy knit white crewneck sweater, a little yellowed with age, with a royal-blue "SHS" in the middle, for Springfield High School. Underneath the "SHS," embroidered in small letters, was "Captain."

"It still fits," Blister's mother said, sinking down on the flowered chintz couch, her face wet with tears.

CHAPTER TWELVE

Something happened to Blister when her mother came into the living room in her cheerleading clothes. One moment she had been standing in the middle of the room, her arms tight across her chest, full of happiness to hear her mother's voice, to see Mary Reed walk into the living room alive and safe. And the next moment, she was breathless with anger.

"You've got to stop crying, Mama," she said, her voice shaking, the veins in her neck pale-blue and protruding. "And take off those stupid clothes."

Mary Reed looked up, wiped the wetness off her face with the palm of her hand.

"I *hate* the way you look dressed up like you're fifteen," Blister said. "And I hate that you lie around the apartment like you're going to be dead by the time I get home from school."

Daisy G. had rushed over to the stove and was making hot chocolate, taking angel food cake out of the bread box, and cutting it in squares.

"We need something to eat," she was saying. "We're all too tired and hungry and bad-tempered."

"I'm not tired at all, or even hungry," Blister said. "I'm perfectly fine — but I could've been killed walking home from school, with nobody at home to see whether I got there or not. And you wouldn't have known the difference."

"I thought you were with your father," Mary Reed said. "He told me he was going to pick you up after school and take you out to dinner."

"Well, Big Surprise, he didn't pick me up," Blister said. "So I was walking home, thinking of course you'd be there on the couch as usual, or asleep in bed. Anything could have happened to me if Daisy G. hadn't just driven by."

"I'm so sorry, Alyssa," Mary Reed said. "But I got up this morning feeling the same old terrible I've been feeling for weeks and found the ring you'd so sweetly given me. Then I thought that maybe if I came over to Daisy G.'s and looked through all my old scrapbooks, and remembered what I used to be like when I was young, then I'd feel better."

"And you do, don't you, Mary?" Daisy G. said handing her a cup of hot chocolate and some angel food cake. "Don't you feel better now?"

"She's crying," Blister said, pouring herself some hot chocolate. "She can't feel that much better. I *hate* that you cry all the time in that whimpery voice."

"Sometimes I can't help it," her mother said.

"You can so help it, Mama. Or at least you could go see a doctor who could help you feel better," Blister said, wandering into her grandmother's bedroom, turning on the light.

The room was a mess, clothes all over the floor: coats and dresses and skirts that her mother must have been trying on. Daisy G.'s bed was covered with Mary Reed's photographs and scrapbooks and dried corsages and athletic awards and autograph books and letters. Blister slid into a chair and put her hands over her ears, so that she didn't have to listen to her mother's voice.

"What's the trouble?" Daisy G. asked, rushing into the bedroom with a plate of cake.

Blister shrugged, shaking her head at the offer of cake. "Nothing."

"Nothing?" Daisy G. sat down on the edge of the chair.

"Well, something is the matter, of course," Blister said. "And it's not just her crying and sleeping all day — but worse than anything, I don't like seeing Mama in her cheerleading outfit."

"Don't fret about that," Daisy G. said. "Mary wanted to find out if she was still the same size. Women are like that."

"That's not the truth and you know it's not, and so do I," Blister said, quietly. "The truth is my mother's in terrible trouble."

Later, Daisy G. parked her car in the lot outside Jack Reed's apartment, Mary beside her, Blister in the backseat.

"You were right about what you said about my being in trouble, Alyssa," Mary said, turning around to talk to Blister.

"Isn't there anything you can do about it?" Blister asked.

"I think there is something I can do," her mother said. "I can go to the doctor who took care of me this summer, when I was so upset, and maybe he can help me get better."

"Maybe he can. I hope so," Blister said.

"That's a very good idea, Mary," Daisy G. said. "Of course he can help. That's his job. You should call him tomorrow."

"I don't want to be like this, Alyssa," Mary Reed told her. "More than anything, I want to be back to my old self."

"And you think you can be?" Blister asked.

"I think I can." She reached in her pocket and took out the gold ring Blister had left for her as a gift that morning.

"I loved that you wanted me to have this ring, sweetheart."

"I'm glad."

"The only problem is that it isn't my ring."

"It is now."

"I'd like you to take it upstairs and give it to your father."

"I don't want to do that," Blister said. "I want to go home."

"Your father is in the apartment. Look. I can see him walking back and forth across the living room," her mother said.

Blister looked up. In the window, his back to them, in a turtleneck and jeans, was Jack Reed. He was talking on the telephone.

"If you think I'm taking the ring back to him, you're wrong," Blister said.

"All you have to do is go upstairs, knock on the door, and hand it to him," her mother said. "You don't have to talk to him, and you don't have to say you're sorry."

"I'm not sorry," Blister said.

"That's fine. But you did take the ring, Alyssa, and you have to return it," Mary Reed said.

"I gave the ring to you," Blister said. "If you don't want it, *you* give it back to him."

Daisy G. turned off the car engine, and they sat quietly in the dark, Blister looking out the window at the long shaft of yellow from the streetlight.

"If you're waiting for me," she said, finally, "I'm not getting out of the car."

"I really don't understand why she has to do this, Mary," Daisy G. said.

Blister's mother was quiet, her hands folded in her lap, staring straight ahead.

"I want Alyssa to return it."

"Just that?" Daisy G. asked.

Blister was silent, slipping down in the backseat, hoping her father, if he happened to look out the window, wouldn't see her.

"It's because Alyssa took the ring, Daisy G.," Mary Reed said. "I don't want her to be the one in the wrong."

"I'll go with you, Alyssa," Daisy G. said. "Let's get it over with."

And she hopped out of the front seat, opening the back door. Blister had no choice.

"I'm not giving back the clothes," she said to her mother. "I *need* them for school." She followed Daisy G. up the steps to her father's apartment.

At the landing, they could hear music playing. They had to knock twice before Jack Reed heard that anyone was there.

He was dressed and barefooted when he opened the door. Behind him, on the couch in the living room, her tiny feet on the coffee table and reading a magazine, was the young woman who must have been Tamara.

"Alyssa!" His face was white.

"I brought this back." Blister reached out and put the ring in her father's hand.

He was stepping out into the hall.

"I need to talk to you," he said to Blister.

"I have to go home now," Blister said, already dashing down the steps to the first floor. "Maybe next week, if I have the time."

"So I guess you saw that," Blister said, slipping her hand in Daisy G.'s as they walked to the car.

"Tootsie?"

"Tamara."

"I saw that. We can't jump to conclusions."

"I can."

"Well, I wouldn't worry about other people's lives, Alyssa. You can't do anything about them."

"We can't fix it between Dad and Mama, is what you're saying?"

"It doesn't look that way," Daisy G. said.

"At least I'm not going to spend all my time wishing things were different."

That night Blister couldn't get to sleep. Outside her room, Daisy G. and her mother were talking, too low for her to hear what was being said, but loud enough to keep her awake. She tried to concentrate on the assembly tomorrow morning, picturing the principal with the list of new cheerleaders, the auditorium full of students, every class in attendance, every teacher.

But each time Blister imagined the assembly, her mother's voice interrupted her thoughts and she remembered that she was in this new apartment which she hated, with her father gone off — probably for good — her mother miserable, sleeping day and night.

And in the slice of time between waking and sleeping, just after nine o'clock, Daisy G. talking in the background of Blister's mind, she suddenly understood why she had been upset to see her mother dressed as a girl. She got out of bed and went into the living room.

"I know why I hated to see you in your old cheerleading uniform."

"Why is that?" Mary Reed said.

"Because you're my mother and a grown-up," Blister said.

"You're right, of course," Mary Reed said, softly.

"I want you to be like you used to be before everything happened," Blister said.

"In time, I will be, Alyssa. Slowly, but I will be myself again."

Back in her room, Blister turned off her light and climbed into bed with a powerful sense of relief, falling almost immediately asleep.

CHAPTER THIRTEEN

It was still dark when Blister woke up and scrambled through Tamara's remaining clothes for the black T-shirt with TROUBLE written on the front. Then she put on her own red trousers and sneakers and a sweatshirt embroidered with "Bixley Elementary" tied around her waist. She spread Tamara's clothes out on the bed, the slinky skirt, the tiny gauzy tops, the navy-blue dress, and the short strapless, the skinny little T-shirts in bright colors. She took two

T-shirts: one orange, with glitter around the neck; the other fuchsia, with a dragon in bright red on the back. The rest of the clothes she stuffed in a paper bag, taped the bag shut, and wrote a note to her father which she clipped to the top of the bag:

Dear Dad,

I have kept three T-shirts, including the one with TROUBLE *written on it, but the rest is here. I think I deserve the T-shirts. Maybe I'll see you next week, but I won't be spending any more weekends in your apartment. Mama is fine now — completely fine — not even mad about Tamara. But I'm mad, which is why I'm keeping the* TROUBLE *T-shirt as a souvenir.*

Yours sincerely,

Blister

P.S. You might be interested to know that Mama is completely fine. She even had her hair cut like it was before she met you.

Daisy G. was in the kitchen making hot chocolate, doing one of her little dance steps with a chair, lifting her leg on top of the back of the chair.

Blister dropped the orange and fuchsia T-shirts on the kitchen table.

"One's for you and one's for Mama," she said.

"I think I want the one with the dragon," Daisy G. said, putting it on over her nightshirt.

Blister poured herself cereal and milk, eating quickly.

"So today's the day," her mother said, coming into the kitchen.

"I'm pretty worried, but I think I'm going to make the squad," Blister said.

"I'll keep my fingers crossed."

She kissed her mother good-bye.

"I've left the stuff for Dad by the front door, and put a message on his machine asking him to pick it up."

"I'm glad you did that, Alyssa." Mary Reed followed her daughter down the steps to the first floor of the apartment building.

"Are you very mad at him?"

Her mother shook her head.

"What happened is both of our faults."

"Well, I don't like him right now."

"But you will again."

Blister shrugged.

"Maybe," she said. Then she saw Jess walk by across the street, and she dashed out of the building to catch up with her.

*   *   *

All day, the fifth-grade candidates for the cheerleading squad were jittery. They giggled and laughed, unable to concentrate in their classes. They sat at the same table in the cafeteria, but they didn't feel like eating lunch. Mary Sue threw up again and even Bylynda, cool as a cucumber as Daisy G. would say, had to go to the nurse's office to get something for her stomachache. By the time assembly came around, it was two o'clock, and Blister was a wreck.

The announcements in assembly took forever. The bake sales and car washes and Christmas contributions and music concerts and athletic competitions went on and on. And then there was a collection for Mr. Barnstable, the janitor, and his family, who had lost their house in a fire. And then a member of the North Haven police force was there to talk about the dangers of the street, warning them about talking to strangers, or walking about after dark, or leaving their bicycles unlocked, or hanging out near the high school, because drugs were sometimes sold there.

When the time for the announcement of the fifth- and sixth-grade cheerleading squad came, Blister was sitting next to Barbie and Mary Sue, and Mary Sue had grabbed her hand. She was just beginning to feel that she was going to die of oxygen deprivation when the principal and gym teacher walked to the front of the auditorium. Ms. Hartman gave a long speech about the tradition of cheerleaders at Bixley Elementary, about how they were chosen to bolster the spirit of the teams and the students, about how many qualified girls tried out, and how sad it was that all of them could not be chosen.

"I wish she'd shut up," Mary Sue said. "I'm going to wet my pants."

"Me too," Barbie whispered across to her.

And finally Ms. Hartman opened the piece of paper she was holding, pulled the microphone close to her mouth, and began.

"When I read your names, I would like you to come to the front of the auditorium and stand next to me to receive your letter sweater with 'Bixley' on the front."

"I can't listen," Mary Sue said.

"Me neither," Barbie said.

The principal cleared her throat. "There are five fifth-graders. Would the following girls please come forward.

Veronique Galleaux.

Mary Sue Otter.

Bylynda Revere.

Jess Mahoney.

Barbie Sachs."

The auditorium turned dark as the inside of a cave, and the sound of clapping, of cheers and piercing screams seemed to come from the deep center of a glass bottle. Blister couldn't breathe.

It was a hundred years before the assembly was dismissed — hours walking in a line down the side of the auditorium, with her almost-friends murmuring to her, some whispering to each other.

"I can't believe you didn't make it," Bylynda said. "You were really good."

"Thanks," Blister said, her lips fixed, her eyes dry, her powerful defense system in gear.

"Oh, Blister, I'm so so sorry," Anne said. "You were so good."

"Sorry about you too," Blister said.

"Oh I knew I wouldn't make it. I'm just too slow."

"Call me tonight," Bylynda said to Blister, as she packed up her locker.

"Call me too," Veronique said.

Sara Barton crept up to the side of Blister, whispering in her ear.

"Like I said, it's a popularity contest."

Blister held her expression intact. Not smiley, not too sweet — an expression that betrayed nothing — counting the seconds until she reached the doors to the auditorium, running through what she would do: go to her locker, get her books and coat, her gym clothes, go to homeroom to be dismissed; go to the drugstore to buy M&M's and Hershey's Kisses, and maybe more candy to stash under her pillow for comfort. She was concentrating so hard that she didn't even see her mother leaning against the wall of the auditorium with Daisy G.

"I feel terrible for you," her mother said, as they walked down Market Street, on their way to the ice-cream shop for a hot-fudge sundae with whipped cream.

"I was the best," Blister said. "I know that."

"I know you were," her mother said, reaching down to take her hand.

"It wasn't exactly fair."

"No, it wasn't fair. And this year hasn't been fair to you — nor have I. I've been worrying too much about my own sadness, and not enough about yours. You should be angry, instead of resilient."

"'Elastic,'" Blister said, walking between her mother and grandmother into the late afternoon's descending sun, thinking she would prefer a butterscotch sundae instead of chocolate, thinking she'd call Bylynda and ask her for a sleepover. Or invite Veronique for Saturday night. Maybe she'd invite them both to go bowling.

"'Elastic' is what Daisy G. says about me."

About the Author

SUSAN SHREVE "has a spectacular gift for taking ordinary youngsters and making them do extraordinary things" (*The Philadelphia Inquirer*). Her novels for children and adults include *Jonah the Whale and How He Became Incredibly Famous*; *Ghost Cats*; *The Flunking of Joshua T. Bates*; *The Gift of the Girl Who Couldn't Hear*; and *The Visiting Physician*. She is a professor of English at George Mason University in Washington, D.C.